I0682444

No Matter What

A novel by Algernon Tucker

No Matter What © 2016 by Algernon A. Tucker
Correspondence: admin@AchieversCourse.com
Website: AchieversCourse.com/nomatterwhat
Phone: 404-532-9163

Send all requests to **admin@AchieversCourse.com.** L.I.F.E.$.T.Y.L.E. and Life$TYLE are registered trademarks of Achievers Course Enterprises.

Limit of Liability/Disclaimer of Warranty: While the publisher and author have used their best efforts in preparing this book, they make no representations or warranties with respect to the accuracy or completeness of the contents of this book and specifically disclaim any implied warranties of merchantability or fitness for a particular purpose.

No warranty may be created or extended by sales representatives or written sales material. The advice and strategies contained herein may not be suitable for your situation. You should consult with a professional where appropriate.

Neither the publisher nor author shall be liable for any loss of profit or any other commercial damages, including but not limited to special, incidental, consequential, or other damages.

Sales: For information regarding bulk purchases, please contact Achievers Course Enterprises by phone at **404-532-9163**.

Library of Congress Cataloging-in-Publication Data
Tucker, Algernon A.
No Matter What: a novel / Algernon A. Tucker
     p. cm.
1. Intimate Relationships – Fiction 2. Spirituality – Fiction. 3.
     Entrepreneurship – Fiction 4. Divorce – Fiction I. Title

ISBN 10: 0692268308
ISBN 13: 9780692268308

Printed in the United States of America
    10 9 8 7 6 5 4 3 2 1

Dreamtimes Photographer Credits: John Blanton, Flashon Studio, Imagery Majestic, Sophie Phelps, Terence Mendoza, Kristian Sekulic, Shailesh Nanal, Aleksandar Todorovic, Frank Herzog, and Yann Poirier (**www.dreamstime.com**)

Cover Photographer Credit: Sam Jasper Photography

Table of Contents

Prologue

Still Waiting, Still Hopeful

September 17, 1999

Sixty seconds is all it took. My excitement . . . *annihilated*. My heart pounded like a kick drum. Protective instinct led the attack. Jackson, help me. Her innocence stripped away. I fought to reclaim it, to redeem myself. This decision nearly destroyed her, although the blood on my hands suggested he was the victim.

Given the circumstances of this painful experience and the opportunity to decide again, I wouldn't change a thing except her last name . . . *and Reidsville*.

Geovana's poetry comforts me. During the last nine years, it's kept me hopeful that one day nature will guide her back into my arms. My love for her is permanent. This is my promise. Amen.

Chapter 1

The Power of Words

Jackson's Influence Expands

I'll never forget that day. I couldn't believe what I was hearing. Every word he spoke seemed to be directed toward me and people who look like me. If only I had known sooner how deeply this would cut, perhaps I would have changed my thinking long ago.

It happened on January 8, 2000. I'd been a member of Toastmasters for about five years and had heard many great things about the Charismatic Communicators Toastmasters Club in Decatur, Georgia.

What impressed me most about this club was the number of phenomenal speakers they'd developed, who now earned at least $5,000 per speaking engagement. Determined to sharpen my skills, I decided to visit the Charismatic Communicators.

When the big day rolled around, I was pumped. Since it was about a forty-five-mile drive and the meeting started at 9:00am, I got up early enough to leave by 7:15am. This would give me plenty of time to stop for breakfast.

The sky was a clear, deep blue, and the sun had gently penetrated the horizon. Its bright orange color confidently resided in the place where darkness appeared only an hour earlier. Geese flew overhead in V-formation, making their obnoxiously wonderful sound.

I started the car and backed out of the driveway. The soothing sounds of Najee were playing, causing my mind and body to relax. I absolutely love jazz music.

At Pleasant Hill, I exited the highway and made a left turn. The drive-through was busy at Chick-Fil-A, so I parked and went inside to order.

I sat down, thanked the Father, and took a bite of my burrito. While sitting there, I began to imagine what I could do with all the money I was going to earn as a professional speaker. If I booked three speeches a month at five thousand per speech, I would generate one hundred and eighty thousand annually. Add to this the sale of books and audio CDs, and I'd be set financially. I pondered, "What new options would I have with the increased cash flow? What investments should I make for an enjoyable retirement?"

Expensive cars and jewelry fascinated me. But thoughts of my dream home kept me awake at night. During the previous year, I'd visited the Sugarloaf Country Club with a realtor, to help me visualize my dream home. I acquired the blueprints and hoped to build within five years. The Toastmasters meeting launched the chain of events, which positioned me to move forward with my plans.

At 8:00am, I proceeded south on Interstate 85. The traffic was lighter than usual. I thought to myself, "I hope the roads are clear," because I wanted to arrive early. As I approached Spaghetti Junction, I moved into the lane for 285 east and continued my forty-five-mile journey to Decatur.

When I walked into the building, I was greeted by the most beautiful black woman I'd ever seen. Her caramel brown skin, thick red lips, seductive smile, low-cut jeans, and vivacious curves put me in a trance. Each word she spoke massaged my ears like thirty minutes alone in the car with Sade, singing "Smooth Operator."

She smiled and then introduced herself as Sasha. I paused to acknowledge my appreciation. Sasha looked spectacular. I said, "Hello Sasha, my name is Psoloman Blacksmith." She asked, "Is this your first time visiting our club?" I responded, "Yes it is." Sasha reached for an information and membership packet and said, "Be sure to come and see me before you leave. I'm the VP of Membership." While nodding my head in agreement, I thought, "I wonder if she's free for lunch."

Then another attractive woman placed her hand on my shoulder, causing me to snap out of the spell Sasha had cast upon me. She introduced herself as the club president and said, "You're sitting up front with me."

We chatted for a few minutes and then the meeting was called to order. According to the meeting agenda, three speakers were scheduled for presentations.

The Toastmaster introduced the first speaker, Mr. Jackson Gray. His speech, titled "We Are Worthy of Respect and Admiration" was one of the best presentations I had ever witnessed. It was also the most disconcerting. His penetrating delivery and relentless resolve awakened not only my deepest love, but also my greatest fear. I hated him and, at the same time, admired his power and confidence.

Brown-skinned with a muscular build, hazel eyes, and a goatee, he stood at the lectern, ready for battle, certain and poised. His appearance was striking and professional - black tailored-suit, red bow tie, and a million-dollar smile. I could feel the respect he'd earned with this audience, and I wanted it for myself. He commanded their attention through silence for nearly thirty seconds, and then his voice boomed like thunder.

If I could buy you *for what you think you're worth* and then sell you *for your true value,* I'd make a fortune. Mr. Toastmaster, fellow Toastmasters, and Honored Guests, my name is Jackson Gray, and I have a monumental problem to solve. It's a problem designed to rob you of the essential skills needed to pursue happiness and live life to the fullest. Even so, you don't have to be its victim. There is a way of thinking and living which cultivates these skills, bringing wealth and freedom to your doorstep. Does anyone know what it's like to be free? I do, and today I'm extending the invitation to you.

Before we get into the lesson, there are two questions I hope you'll consider during my presentation. The first question: What is the secret to creating wealth? And the second: How does wealth relate to freedom?

My interest in economics began to take shape around age nine when my mother became an entrepreneur and gave me a book titled The Richest Man In Babylon. Studying the book's financial principles produced a desire to know more about the science of money. Mom would always tell me, "God blesses the child that's got his own." As a result, I've done well financially. However, my black brothers and sisters remain in financial ruin, indicating my work is not complete. I'm positive I have the solution and appreciate you allowing me to share my wealth-building plan.

Four years ago, I received a letter which helped me understand the process used to keep the general population of black people poverty-stricken, pretentious, and petrified. When I opened the letter, page one prepared me for this remarkable assignment. It read, "Make sure that your mind is clear when you sit down to review this document. The reason I'm sharing this with you is because you have the desire and skill to reverse the damaging effects caused by the process explained on the following pages. Study with this idea in mind and I guarantee you will leave a powerful legacy.

And remember, economic position and strength are the motivating factors. It's *never been about racism*. I've written this statement at the top of every page as a reminder. Be strong, young brother. I believe in you."

Initially, intense anger made it difficult for me to see anything positive about the letter's content. It kept my wounds open and my mind distracted. I'd read a paragraph at a time, and then put it away for several days. The words overwhelmed my soul with a desire for revenge. If not for the weekly conversations with my teacher, I'd still be angry. He persuaded me to look at the letter's content through the eyes of leadership and management, defining leadership as *influence* and management as *control*. He said, "Without influence and control, it is impossible to build wealth."

Thinking about this statement daily inspired me to conduct the first of many leadership surveys. I chose one hundred men and women working in various capacities of leadership – politicians, chief executive officers, ministers, educators, and coaches. It took six months to complete, and I asked each of them the same question:

What motivates a person, who is serving in a leadership capacity or authoritative role, to purposefully create obstacles and hardships for subordinates who seek financial success and economic independence?

Dr. Claud Anderson - America's finest African-American scholar on the subject of economics – provided the most stimulating response. Instead of recommending a fix for the self-serving leader, he proposed independence for the employee or subordinate. Dr. Anderson suggested that "The secret to creating wealth and becoming free is to own and control resources. There is no wealth potential in a job. It is the owner and producer of the job who have the wealth potential."

He advised, "When a group or community begins to acquire resources and manage them for the economic benefit of the group, they have created an economy, a mechanism to produce income, wealth, jobs, and business opportunities."

Both Dr. Anderson and I agree that white America has done a number on us. Their early system of dehumanizing and psychological conditioning left black people divided, apprehensive, and fearful. One hundred and thirty five years legally emancipated, we still think like slaves, living our lives according to self-imposed restrictions.

To change this reality, we must unite on the basis of economic influence and control. Dr. Anderson advised, "When a *group or community* begins to acquire resources and manage them. . ." He did not say, "Go at it alone." There's no place for the lone ranger, independent thinker, or soloist in the wealth-building plan I propose today. A new kind of black leader must emerge; one who understands the value of teamwork and is encouraged, rather than intimidated, by the white man's economic position and strength. The white business elite are not to be feared, but studied and in many ways, imitated.

I froze when he looked fiercely into my eyes, as if to say, "How dare you show up at this meeting?" Mr. Gray's implied question made me feel so uncomfortable that I considered leaving. It seemed like every eye in the room was staring at me. His non-verbal interrogation caused me to examine my motivation for attending, as well as my contribution to the problem he'd described.

He continued by asking, "Who has read or heard about the *Willie Lynch Letter*?" A small percentage of the predominantly African-American audience raised their hands. A handful of Latinos and Asians sat quietly, captivated.

Faces contorted, tears began to fall, and hands covered mouths as he read a section of the *Willie Lynch Letter*. A blend of heart-clenching emotions – *shame, guilt, humiliation, fear, and disappointment* – intensified in my gut as Mr. Gray described physical and psychological torture. I felt like a criminal, an accessory to murder, simply because I looked like the facilitators of terror described in the letter.

Mr. Gray stepped from behind the lectern and took a seat, facing the audience. Smiling, he panned the room, aligning eyes and hearts to his own. The men moved to the edge of their seats, hands cupping their chins, while the women relished this defining moment. A firm, yet affectionate sound filled the room when Jackson spoke.

Ralph Waldo Emerson said, "Our chief want is someone who will inspire us to be what we know we could be." John Kenneth Galbraith said, "All of the great leaders have had one characteristic in common: it was the willingness to confront unequivocally the major anxiety of their people in their time." This class of leadership, I now extend to you. I charge you with the responsibility of leaving an inheritance, a bridge, and an example which refuses to be ignored.

My wealth-building plan begins with a twenty-one week study of leadership principles. The resource I've selected to guide us through this transformation is titled The 21 Most Powerful Minutes of a Leader's Day by John C. Maxwell. This book provides an illustration of great and not-so-great techniques and strategies used by biblical characters in positions of leadership. Completing the daily lessons will prepare us to cultivate quality relationships and equip us to establish the foundation for a phenomenal life of service to others – the wealth building cornerstone.

In closing, I say to the black men, know that your history presents some of the finest contributors to the advancement of society. Let their accomplishments be a source of inspiration, as we proceed to build a powerful and wealthy nation. Join forces with other great men and women, and then prove to the world that we are worthy of respect and admiration.

Mr. Toastmaster.

I excused myself from the meeting early. It was a long drive home. So much to consider; where would I start? "How could one man bear such a heavy burden?" I thought. The truth is I felt as though I was Willie Lynch.

After careful thought and prayer, God showed me how to redirect my ambition in a way to serve humanity. He told me to study First Corinthians Twelve, because it contained the secret. God also made it clear to take instruction only from Him during the initial phase of my training.

I discovered in First Corinthians Twelve the necessity for and benefits of our differences. God taught me about building multi-cultural teams.

For the next eight years, He prepared me for this assignment through a series of relationships, books, small groups, audio lessons, and religious doctrines. Dale Carnegie's How To Win Friends and Influence People has remained a source of inspiration and instruction, as I strive to be of greater value and influence.

The journey has been long and difficult, but I'm thankful that God chose me. He even sent friends to comfort me, expand my perspective, and make life meaningful. I value these relationships with my life and take time each day to let them know how much I appreciate their love, support, and friendship.

Psoloman Blacksmith

Chapter 2

The Things We Do

Jackson's Love For Geovana

New York Times bestselling author and speaker Jackson Gray has been touring the country for the past eighteen months conducting seminars based on his first book, <u>My Money Works For Me</u>. The book has sold more than one million copies and is currently being translated into three languages.

The December 16, 2003 issue of *Essence Magazine* covered an article about Jackson titled "When The Student Is Ready." The story read:

I was eighteen at the time. Geovana and I had been dating for three years. Both of us were excited about graduating in a few weeks. We were ready for the college experience and our opportunity to change a segment of society. Geovana was accepted at Spelman College in the Sociology and Anthropology Degree Program, and I was accepted at Morehouse College in the Economics Degree Program.

I knew from the moment I saw her that Geovana would be my wife. The way she spoke to my soul was something that I've never been able to describe with words. She had an amazing ability to captivate audiences through her fluid mastery of the English language, particularly through spoken word. Geovana began developing this gift shortly after her best friend's parents divorced.

I clearly remember the night Geovana delivered her verbal masterpiece. We were out at the Urban Café for open mic and poetry night. That evening represented the beginning of our journey toward a happily-ever-after. However, my plan to propose a lifelong commitment was interrupted. I'd been saving for two years to purchase her engagement ring.

Geovana's introduction was classic. The emcee referred to her as, "The Wisdom That God Made." People were amazed by her eloquence and the richness of her spoken thoughts. Her age indicated youth, but wisdom proved to be her guiding light.

Geovana was determined to help women communicate more effectively, particularly with the men in their lives. Her dream was to create a practical solution for keeping relationships strong and families together.

A breathtaking and flawlessly-dressed Geovana stood up and walked to the stage. She wore a sexy, long, black and elegant halter dress. The dress was cut in a u-shape, her breasts slightly exposed in the center. A heart-shaped pendant rested just beneath her breasts, seductively drawing you into her world. Geovana's peanut butter brown skin was as smooth as silk and her smile electrifying. The slit in her dress exposed the lower portion of her thigh, adding just the right amount of flash to drive the men in the crowd wild and make the ladies run to the mirror.

The music began to play and Geovana stepped up to the microphone. In a strong, yet massaging tone she said, "The title of this poem is *Masculine Virginity*. I dedicate this to my man JD, Jackson Dwayne Gray, who turned eighteen today. Happy Birthday, Baby! Ladies, I know you will appreciate the words to this expression of my soul. As for the men, don't let the title fool you; JD satisfies me completely."

Geovana began to recite the poem over the sexy jazz selection from Dave Koz titled "You Are Me, I Am You."

> Masculine, his voice deep like the ocean floor,
>
> Always ready to give me more!
>
> Satisfaction . . .
>
> When expressing his love my man is never lacking!

In a physical throw down,

He can take me the full twelve rounds!

Making love to my mind,

Oh . . .

You thought I was talking about from behind!

Well he's got that too, but this poem is not about the P-U . . .

But the connection,

The bridge between our minds an erection,

His masculinity, it is perfection!

Never does he give me reason to wonder,

About another woman coming to steal my thunder.

Penetration,

The honey comb of my mind is his destination!

His words . . . they massage my ears,

I say to him . . . slow and easy my dear,

I'm not going anywhere.

Do you think I'd give up this moment in time?

To settle for a silver dime,

When you're a silver dollar,

To the end of this life it is you that I follow.

So come here to mama!

I was completely taken by the seductive tone in which she expressed the unbreakable connection between her soul and mine. I had never experienced this side of Geovana. It was simply amazing.

She thanked the audience for listening and received a standing ovation. The ladies cheered. I felt like the man of the century. Tears began to form in my eyes, but my masculinity kept them inside. I walked up to Geovana, embraced her intimately, and gave her a passionate kiss. I can still taste her, even after all these years. At that moment, it was as if heaven came to earth and rested with me and Geovana. But this feeling didn't last for long.

Geovana walked to the ladies room to freshen up, and I walked back to our table. A few minutes later, I heard Geovana yell, "Get your hands off of me." I jumped out of my seat and ran toward her.

When I came around the corner, I couldn't believe my eyes. A white man from the audience had his hand under Geovana's dress. I lost it! The distressed look on her face was like a sword being thrust into my heart. Just moments before, she had seen me as her protector, as her king. Now, I watched as he violated the woman I love. I had to stop him.

I nearly beat him to death. Had I been carrying a knife, I would have cut off the hand he used to touch Geovana's innocence. Not even I had been permitted to touch her there. That night was supposed to be our first time making love. Seconds later, I was tackled from behind and handcuffed.

The white man turned out to be an undercover police officer. Although no drugs were actually found on the scene, the sting operation gave him grounds to frisk Geovana and the other women. I was so engrossed by what he was doing to Geovana that I didn't even notice the other ladies lined up against the wall.

I was sentenced to five years and sent to Georgia State Prison in Reidsville, Georgia. I was convicted for assault and battery of a police officer, attempted murder, and interfering with a police investigation. The judge's final words still haunt me in my dreams, "Boy, I'm sending you to a place that you'll never forget." Reidsville housed the most recalcitrant and aggressive adult male offenders in the Georgia Prison System. This place proved to be hell on earth.

Because of the three-hour drive from Atlanta, Geovana only visited twice a month. However, she sent me poems and letters every day. Mail call had a way of revealing that the men locked down in prison were still human. They still had feelings and needed love. Geovana's letters and visits literally kept me alive during the first year of my incarceration.

During one visit, I told her about the violations often experienced by new inmates: the beatings, rapes, and murders. Geovana knew intuitively I'd been assaulted by another prisoner and began crying uncontrollably. The crying turned into screaming, which alarmed the guards. She was asked to leave. Her letters arrived less frequently with fewer words. Months went by before I saw her again.

Geovana did her best to stand by me, but I guess it became too much to bear. She was so disgusted by the horror of prison life, she couldn't take it anymore. Prison had begun transforming me into a beast of a man. Thoughts of losing her dominated my mind.

Then the inevitable happened. The pressures of school, her father, and youth gradually caused Geovana to cave in. I received a final letter explaining that our relationship was over. I'd hoped that our engagement would preserve the relationship, knowing that I couldn't offer her what he'd begun providing.

I nearly lost my mind. I stopped caring about life and adopted an "I don't give a you know what" attitude during the following six months. I rebelled and spent many hours in solitary confinement. Then an inmate serving a life sentence saw my downward spiral and took me under his wing. His name is Mr. Clyde Richardson and he was forty years old at the time. He had been incarcerated for ten years, since July 1980, serving a life sentence for charges similar to my own. The man who violated his wife hadn't been so lucky.

Mr. Richardson knew he would never leave this place, but wanted me to be free. Wisdom had taught him that it's not the chains and bars which enslave us, but the point of view we adopt while serving time. Mr. Richardson saw that I was headed toward a lifetime in the prison system if I did not begin to change my thinking.

From our conversations, Mr. Richardson learned that I was intellectually strong and had a passion for economics, banking, and business ownership. Though I had forfeited the full scholarship to attend Morehouse, I still had a burning desire to pursue my passion. I later realized that God sent Mr. Richardson to help me redirect my life. Our first stop on the journey was his personal library.

He insisted that I learn about and thoroughly understand the legal system, the life and legacy of Malcolm X, and principles for success in life and business. The four books most significant in my transformation were: The Best Defense by Alan M. Dershowitz, The Autobiography of Malcolm X by Alex Haley, Think and Grow Rich: A Black Choice by Dennis Kimbro and Law of Success by Napoleon Hill.

The strong thinking skills which I developed as a result of studying these books saved me from dying in the pits of hell - better known as prison. Malcolm X convinced me that there's life after prison. Dennis Kimbro professed that whatever the mind of a black man can conceive and believe, he can achieve. Alan Dershowitz taught me that in this country, you're guilty until proven innocent. Finally, Napoleon Hill illustrated the power of forming a mastermind alliance with others and having a clearly defined reason for living.

Before being convicted, Mr. Richardson was a prominent accountant and financial services agent. He was also on the verge of publishing a breakthrough system to teach middle-income families how to implement the wealth building strategies of the truly wealthy.

During the next three and a half years, he taught me everything he knew and I emerged from prison, an economic genius. I also developed a solid understanding of the legal system. With a potential best-seller in hand and a desire to change the economic point of view of Middle America, I stepped into my new role with a stunningly focused intention. Just as my first love, Geovana, had set her mind to teach young women about the importance of communication, I'd set my mind on educating young men to understand the difference between wages and profit, as it related to creating wealth and enjoying life.

Mr. Richardson encouraged me to be patient in releasing the book. He said it would happen when the time was right. It took six years for me to develop into the man qualified to carry this responsibility. Mr. Richardson was very pleased to receive his autographed copy of <u>My Money Works For Me</u> and see his name on the cover as the co-author.

Upon my release, I promised Mr. Richardson that I would write and visit often. He insisted that I write, but I was never to return to Reidsville. I honored his request knowing I'd be ripped apart emotionally.

One year after I met Mr. Richardson, I was introduced to a series of lessons known as One Twenty by Rashad Allah. Mr. Richardson approved of the teachings and encouraged me to study One Twenty with the same intensity that I studied Economics and Law.

These lessons, based on the teachings of the Nation of Islam, provided a basis for black men, women, and children to develop a healthy self-image and self-confidence. I became a member of the Five

Percent Nation.   This was my second mastermind alliance; the first was with Mr. Richardson.

The One Twenty contained lessons on mathematics, science, and history. What impressed me most about One Twenty was the Supreme Mathematics and the teaching method of taking it to the people – in the streets, at the store, on the job. Developing this skill proved helpful.   Just about everyone I encountered experienced transformation in some way.

The men of the Five Percent Nation became my family and Mr. Richardson, the father I'd longed for. He advised many of my Five Percent brothers, encouraging us to look out for and stretch one another. This gave us pride, stability, and hope.

The One Twenty lessons revealed my power, opened my eyes to new possibilities, and put me on a course to establish a vision for my life. Growth and experience made it necessary for me to explore beyond the scope of One Twenty

Today, I still practice the Supreme Mathematics because of its universal application. I've also discovered significant value in the Quran and Bible. My understanding of the Bible catapulted after reconnecting with a gentleman named Psoloman Blacksmith earlier this year. Our meeting became the catalyst for me to begin embracing a mature viewpoint about biblical financial principles. Psoloman showed me how to build a relationship with and take my instruction from God.

As a Five Percenter, I was taught that the black man is God. Something about this idea was very attractive in the beginning, but later proved to be insufficient. I now understand that man can be God, if and when he chooses to do things God's way. The Bible speaks of this in John chapter 15, using a vine and branch analogy to represent how God delivers abundance and positions men and women to represent His finest and most attractive attributes. This shift in perspective has freed me from being a slave to my limited experiences, abilities, and desire for personal gain. It has expanded my thinking and increased my options. I'm grateful for Psoloman. He taught me how to connect scripture to scripture, as well as how to become a friend to God.

Jackson is completing the MBA course at Emory University, and then enrolling in the doctorate program for law. He hopes to have his PhD by August 2005. He's been offered several opportunities to teach My Money Works For Me on the university level, using **The Wealth Creation Ladder™** as his teaching model. His book has topped many best-seller lists and can be purchased online at www.amazon.com.

The Wealth Creation
LADDER™

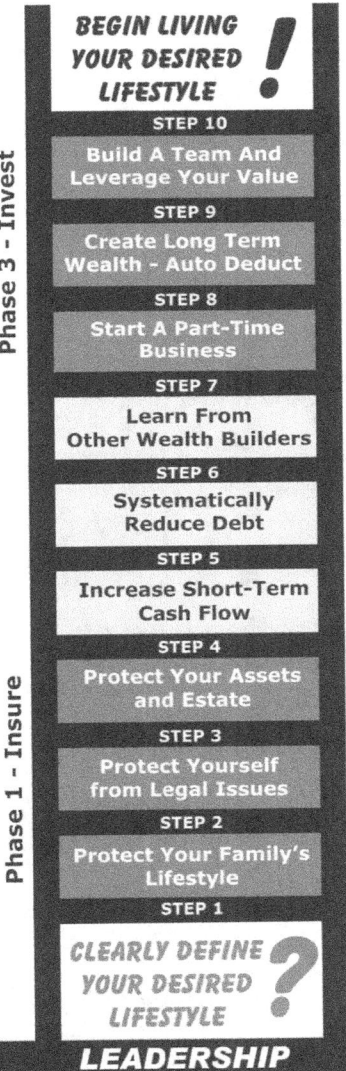

Phase 3 - Invest

BEGIN LIVING YOUR DESIRED LIFESTYLE !

STEP 10
Build A Team And Leverage Your Value

STEP 9
Create Long Term Wealth - Auto Deduct

STEP 8
Start A Part-Time Business

STEP 7
Learn From Other Wealth Builders

STEP 6
Systematically Reduce Debt

STEP 5
Increase Short-Term Cash Flow

Phase 2 - Increase

STEP 4
Protect Your Assets and Estate

STEP 3
Protect Yourself from Legal Issues

STEP 2
Protect Your Family's Lifestyle

STEP 1

Phase 1 - Insure

CLEARLY DEFINE YOUR DESIRED LIFESTYLE ?

LEADERSHIP

Jackson Gray

Chapter 3

The Annual Convention

The Opportunity Psoloman Has Been Waiting For

Toastmasters International
23182 Arroyo Vista
Rancho Santa Margarita, CA 92688
Phone: (949) 858-8255

April 28, 2003

Dear Mr. Blacksmith,

We are excited about the opportunity to kick off the 2003 Annual Toastmasters International 72nd Convention with you as our keynote speaker. You come highly recommended by many of our fine Toastmasters and leaders in the Atlanta area. The purpose of this letter is to provide you information that will assist you in preparing for the Toastmasters Convention. Should you have any questions, please contact the Annual Conventions Department at (949) 858-8255.

The 2003 Annual Toastmasters International 72nd Convention will be hosted in Atlanta, Georgia, August 20, 2003 through August 23, 2003 at the Atlanta Marriot Marquis. Travel, lodging, and dining accommodations have been arranged for you and a guest.

The schedule of events for August 20, 2003, is as follows:

6:00 pm	The Pledge of Allegiance and Invocation
6:05 pm	Opening Ceremony
6:20 pm	A Message From Our President
6:28 pm	Recognition and Awards
6:48 pm	Toastmaster of the Year Presentation
7:00 pm	The Keynote Address (Psoloman Blacksmith)
7:45 pm	Intermission
8:00 pm	Special Guest Speaker (Jackson Gray)
8:15 pm	Special Guest Speaker (Naomi Rhode)
8:30 pm	The Schedule of Events and Closing Remarks
9:00 pm	Black Tie Dinner and Dancing

Enclosed you will find two tickets to the convention, for you and a guest. The attire for Wednesday evening is black tie. Please attend the briefing at 5:00pm on August 20, 2003, in Meeting Room C301 on the first floor of the Atlanta Marriot Marquis. You will be provided updates to the schedule of events and have an opportunity to network with each of the special guest speakers.

Your presentation should be at least thirty-five minutes in length, but should not exceed forty-five minutes. If you plan to provide a handout to the audience, you must submit your handout by May 31, 2003 (in PDF Format) to 2003AnnualConv@toastmasters.org. You are not authorized to solicit business from the audience during your presentation. However, you may set up a product table in the foyer leading to the auditorium and mention the table in your handout.

We at Toastmasters International commend your remarkable achievements as a Professional Communicator and look forward to your keynote address. Thank you for your commitment to make Toastmasters International the cornerstone for the development of exceptional communicators around the world.

Respectfully,

James Simpson

James Simpson, DTM

Chapter 4

Geovana's Surprise

Life In California

Geovana's cell phone rang. She retrieved it from her purse and pressed the green button. The phone slipped from her hand, ejecting the cover and battery as it hit the ground. Geovana checked the screen and found no cracks. It rang again a few minutes later.

Hello!

    Geo, it's Shari. What's up, girl? How you doing?

I'm so glad you called. Just preparing for your visit to California. We're going to have a blast!

    Did you hear about Princess Diana dying in a car crash last night?

Yes! That is so terrible. I cannot get the image of her car out of my mind.

    So young and beautiful. I feel bad for her boys.

I know. Could you imagine?

    Anyway! You know that's not the only reason I called. Jackson has been asking about you.

Really?

    All the time, girl. Why don't you give him a call?

Shari, you know I can't. . . I'm married.

    Geo, there's nothing wrong with having a friendship, is there?

Jackson is not just a friend to me. If I start communicating with him, girl, I might end up on Divorce Court.

    Just give him a chance to be a part of your life. Nothing is going to happen through the phone. Besides, you're in L.A. and Jackson is here in Atlanta.

It's too risky. Sometimes I wish that I'd never married Joshua. My dreams, my hopes, my passion! This marriage sucks and Joshua is a complete ass.

What do you mean, Geo? Has he been putting his hands on you again?

Nope. I only had to stab him once. Lately, he's developed a frightening obsession with adult videos. He watches them constantly – the really raunchy ones. Ever since I've stopped participating in his freak show fantasies, he acts as if I don't exist. No sex. No conversation. No I love yous.

Have the two of you considered speaking with a counselor?

I have, but Joshua tells me what he's doing is normal. He says that he has needs and watching the videos satisfy him. At first, I was open to the idea of watching. Oh my gosh! Can you say multiple orgasms? However, the feel good masked the person I was becoming. Before I knew it, I'd committed unthinkable acts. Joshua turned me into a video slut and took delight in having me any way he chose.

Video slut?

Yes! I rationalized watching the videos, thinking it would help us grow closer. Then Joshua convinced me to recreate the scenes. He didn't ask me to do anything raunchy, at first. Intoxicated by the thrill of taboo, I ignored the signs. Joshua gradually incorporated hardcore porn and I agreed to let him record us. Then it hit me.

What happened!

Shari, you have to brace yourself for this one. Are you sure you want to know?

Geo, stop playing around and tell me what happened.

Girl, it started off as a romantic evening at my favorite restaurant in Laguna Beach. Hush Restaurant is about two hours from our home in Malibu, so we left around 6:00pm. When we arrived, a dozen roses decorated our table as a centerpiece. Joshua took one rose from the vase, extended his hand and said, "This rose is a symbol of my love and a sign of my appreciation for you. It is an honor to have you as my wife." We ordered the Maryland Crab Cakes as an appetizer, followed by Nebraska Prime Beef Filet Mignon and, for dessert, the best bread pudding. Well, not quite the best, but almost as good as your mom's.

>You definitely have to take me to this restaurant for dessert while
>I'm visiting in a few weeks. What happened next?

We drove to the beach and sat there for a while. The sound of the waves was calming. Then Joshua began serenading me with the chorus from our wedding song "Just To Be Close To You:"

>Just to be close to you, girl . . .
>Just for the moment,
>Well . . . just for an hour . . .

We sat there in each other's arms and enjoyed the cool breeze from the ocean. There was a full moon in the sky and the temperature was just right for making love on the beach. On the way to the car, Joshua whispered in my ear, "I have another surprise for you when we get home." I smiled and said, "Okay, baby."

>Geo . . . Will you please stop torturing me will all these details?
>What did Joshua do? Tell me, tell me, tell me!

When we arrived home, he said to me, "Baby, why don't you change into something more comfortable. There's a present for you in the drawer where you keep your panties." Shari, you should have seen the silk gown he bought me. When it touched my skin, all kinds of things started moving around inside of me. There was a matching pair of lace slippers with four-inch heels. "Tonight, I will be his sex goddess," I told myself before turning away from the mirror. He was standing at attention when I walked into the den. The fireplace was lit; sounds of Dave Koz filled the atmosphere with the possibility of an amazing night of non-stop lovemaking. I teased him with the tips of my fingers; I tasted him with a kiss from my lips. He quivered and I smiled. I had him exactly where I wanted him.

Geo, you are such a bad girl.

I know. You know what else?

What?

I've always pretended that I was making love to Jackson.

No!

Yes. Jackson is my ultimate fantasy.

Hmmm! Okay. Well let's talk more about Jackson later. Finish telling me about your romantic evening.

We made love for at least three hours. He took his time and explored every inch of my body. Touching, tasting, slowly penetrating. Joshua is a master at intense and deliberate, slow love making. So many men think they need to pound the kitty. They're supposed to make us purr, not roar.

I know what you mean, girl. A quickie has its place, but a man who can make the loving last is a precious commodity.

I was surprised because there were no videos tonight, just Joshua and I, exploring and enjoying one another. Then someone knocked on the door.

Who was it?

A couple that he'd invited over for sexual games.

You've got to be kidding?

No, girl. He expected us to have sex with the other couple.

He wanted you to???

Yes! Ruined the perfect evening.

So. . . Joshua is bisexual?

I'm not sure. He hasn't tried the orgy thing again. Just comes home and goes into that damn room. And he keeps it locked. Why did I marry this asshole? Joshua is definitely not Jackson. I wish I could pretend Joshua out of my life. I don't want a divorce. I just want to be happy. If only I hadn't transferred to UCLA during my junior year. I never should've visited California. Joshua resulted from that bad decision.

Hold on a minute! UCLA was the start of a great friendship.

Yeah! You are the best thing that's happened in California.

What you need to do is get your mind off of what's happening. I'm not one for interfering with relationships, but Joshua hasn't been good to you. Give Jackson a call. Let him assure you that the past is settled. You need a friend and so does Jackson. You know, I was speaking with Jackson last week after Sunday dinner and he shared the most beautiful story. Just before bedtime, every Friday, he bows beside his bed to renew what he calls his promise. It's a special prayer thanking God for freedom, for ideas, and for the opportunity to experience your love again. I asked him, why Friday and he said, "I met Geovana on a Saturday morning, at the library, while studying for final exams. When she looked up and our eyes met, two lives fused, destined for something amazing. I visit this library often to sit in the chair where she sat, to replay the moment which planted an undying love in my heart; a love that pains me daily, yet keeps me expecting her to return, on a Saturday morning, ready to continue the love affair we began so long ago."

Wow! You know I want to call. I just. . . I mean. . . I don't know what to think. Sometimes I wish I didn't have such strong values. Not sure where my conviction was the night I fell for Joshua. I was so lonely. So angry with Jackson, yet so proud to have someone put their life on the line for me. I realize now the depth of Jackson's love, a quality and intensity not available, even from my own father. My father knew this about Jackson. Envious, he pressured me to quit, just as he'd done. Son-of-a-bitch! "I knew something about that boy wasn't right," he'd repeat. Sending me to UCLA masked his true feelings of inadequacy. My mom suggested I stay at Spelman and endure this painful time. She warned me, "Vana, you will regret it. Don't listen to your father. He's wrong about Jackson." He couldn't stand to watch me love another man. Wanted me all to himself when truthfully, I've never loved him. I've despised my father since he walked into my life, three days after my tenth birthday. I didn't know who to follow. My grades started slipping. Pressure in the red zone. I weighed the pros and cons for months. Thought about how it would affect Jackson. Sealed Jackson's letters with my tears. I needed to hear someone affirm me. I needed to be held, to hear an unfamiliar voice tell me I'm valuable and appreciated. I agreed to visit UCLA during the Christmas holiday of eighty-nine, simply to get away. I didn't go there to meet Joshua. I just needed some peace, some space. Joshua acted as a friend, progressively deepening our trust. He was sympathetic towards Jackson and encouraged me to stick it out. Joshua and I spent hours on the phone. Writing letters no longer satisfied. Joshua invited me to visit during spring break and paid for the trip. Nothing romantically happened, but I knew in my heart that I'd crossed the line. There was no turning back. Jackson and I were finished. Looking back, taking the easy path destroyed my innocence and the only man I've ever loved. I don't deserve him. I don't deserve life.

Let's not talk like that. Don't make me get on a plane. You know I will. Maybe it's time for counseling, Geo. I have a friend here in

Atlanta who is a marriage counselor. I'll contact her to see if she has any recommendations for counselors in L.A.

I'll consider it. I know I tell you this all the time, but I'm saying it again. I really, really, really appreciate your friendship. Jackson is lucky to have a cousin like you, and thank you for keeping me informed about him. When this nightmare is over, I'm coming home to Atlanta. I've suffered enough. The guilt eats at me daily. My life was supposed to be significant; I was supposed to make a difference. Jackson and I had big dreams. I should have waited. He probably despises me for leaving him in that prison all alone.

Geo, trust me, Jackson doesn't hold anything against you. Please don't punish yourself. Jackson still loves you and would do anything for another chance to prove his love. Beautiful and successful women approach him all the time and he politely tells them he's already taken. Jackson's heart belongs to you.

Hearing that makes me sad; it also makes me smile. I hope that his dream comes true.

I'm here for you if you need anything. Love you, Geo.

Thanks, Shari. I love you too! I'll call you in a few days!

Geovana Cortez

Chapter 5

I Never Would Have Imagined

Takoda's Rude Awakening

I was born to be an attorney; at least that is what I thought. I made partner with a prestigious firm in four years; I made the Super Lawyers Top 100 List in six years; my financial portfolio was impeccable; I lived in a million-dollar home; and my name, Takoda Yuma, was respected throughout the state of California and around the United States. None of my clients ever walked away feeling defeated and broke.

Since 1990, MBYKT had been the most sought after firm for legally separating men and women whose love for each other had turned sour. In 1997 more than one million couples in the United States had lost their love and compassion for one another and decided to end their marriages. Ninety-two percent of those divorces involved children – children whose lives were turned upside down. Mariella and I were one of those couples.

With so much going for me how could this happen? Not one of my achievements, awards, or status symbols prevented my wife from leaving me and taking the children. I never imagined I would have to live without my family. The experience nearly took me under. I hadn't considered what it meant to experience the pain of divorce, a feeling I now wish on no one.

I met Mariella at the 1984 Summer Olympic Games held in Los Angeles. Mariella was breathtaking. A mutual friend recognized the attraction and introduced us. A month later, I contacted her father, as she'd instructed. It took four additional calls before he agreed to let me date his daughter.

Carlos Garcia-Márquez, Mariella's father, was stern, yet loving and attentive. On January 10, 1960, following the Cuban Revolution led by Fidel Castro, Carlos capitalized on his big opportunity and headed north to United States. Mariella was born two years later in Miami, Florida. Penelope, her older sister, was nine.

Carlos worked fourteen hour days for three years to establish his contracting business. By 1965, the United States sponsored Freedom Flights increased the rate and number of Cuban immigrants fleeing Cuba. Anticipating this huge market, Carlos was ready. His company specialized in building multiple unit dwellings – mostly triplexes and quadraplexes – later expanding to twelve and twenty-four unit apartment houses. Great leadership skills and a passion for multiple streams of income, led Carlos to hire good workers to handle the day-to-day operation. Within seven years, he established enough monthly cash flow to retire from the daily grind and spend more time diversifying his investments and cultivating his family.

In 1970, Carlos and Victoria - a University of Miami history and law professor - began teaching Mariella speech and debate, as well as researching techniques. Two years later, Mariella was introduced to Victoria's inner circle of attorneys and instructors. While exploring their libraries, studying cases, and attending speech and debate competitions, Mariella developed an insatiable interest for civil litigation law. The 1976 Race Relations Act and certain aspects of the Civil Rights Movement set the course for Mariella's career as an attorney. She graduated with honors from Pepperdine University School of Law in June 1986 and passed the California Bar Exam in July. She chose Pepperdine because of its high academic and moral standards, as well as to be closer to Penelope.

As a Christian University, Pepperdine Affirms:

1. That God is.
2. That God is revealed uniquely in Christ.

3. That the educational process may not, with impunity, be divorced from the divine process.
4. That the student, as a person of infinite dignity, is the heart of the educational enterprise.
5. That the quality of student life is a valid concern of the University.
6. That truth, having nothing to fear from investigation, should be pursued relentlessly in every discipline.
7. That spiritual commitment, tolerating no excuse for mediocrity, demands the highest standards of academic excellence.
8. That freedom, whether spiritual, intellectual, or economic, is indivisible.
9. That knowledge calls, ultimately, for a life of service.

Mariella immediately joined a prestigious Los Angeles firm specializing in civil litigation. The firm's employment law practice consisted mostly of representing individuals against huge corporations in claims based on sexual harassment, discrimination, wrongful termination, wage and hour laws; you get the picture. Mariella was "The Lawyer" for the little guy, and she represented each client with excellence.

Being a spectator in the courtroom when Mariella argued a case was simply fascinating. Her tone was never aggressive or forceful. Mariella communicated with finesse and persuasive compassion, in order to draw out the truth. She used a similar style of communication in our home to create a warm and loving environment for our family. Then something happened.

Our problems began in October 1994, three years after our son Ricardo was born. Emily Rene, our firstborn, was four. Mariella and I decided, during her pregnancy with Ricardo, that she would stay home with the children until they entered school. This allowed her time to teach our children the fundamentals and write a book based on research compiled during her senior year of college.

Mariella chose <u>Shattered Lives</u> as the title for her novel. The story depicts a young woman whose life is turned upside down when her mother divorces her father to be with another man. The girl is emotionally devastated when she learns that her mother is out of her life forever. All contact ceases on the day of her mother's departure, leaving a gaping hole where closeness once resided.

The novel was a big hit with teenage girls and women under thirty-five who had lost a parent to divorce. Mariella appeared on the Oprah Winfrey Show in June 1994 with marriage counselor and ordained rabbi, M. Gary Neuman. Oprah recognizes Gary as one of the best psychotherapists in the world. During the show, Gary suggested that tension and anger between parents, not the actual divorce, puts the children at serious risk. He created the Sandcastles Divorce Recovery Program to teach parents how to intelligently take responsibility and continue providing for their children when divorce has divided the family. The young woman in Mariella's book could have benefited greatly from a program like this.

After the show, the emails and letters started pouring in from girls and women around the country. A few months later, Mariella began acting strange. She developed this uncompromising obsession about divorce attorneys being evil people. She claimed that divorce attorneys were the destroyers of the family unit and demanded that I change my profession.

I tried to reason with Mariella, but she was fully persuaded. The compassionate woman I'd married seven years earlier had somehow gotten lost in the novel and stories she had read from the victims of divorce.

I later discovered that the young girl in Mariella's novel was a depiction of her older sister's response to their parents' divorce.

Penelope never recovered from the divorce, which was finalized on April 4, 1968, when Penelope was fifteen. Mariella, being six at the time, was affected in a different way. Her father quickly redirected her attention to academics, recognizing her passion for learning. Carlos was not successful with Penelope. By age twenty-one, Penelope had attempted suicide three times and was admitted to Metropolitan State Hospital near Los Angeles.

Mariella never spoke to me about her parents' divorce. To my surprise, the woman whom I'd first met at our engagement party was actually Mariella's stepmother. I'd assumed that Victoria was Mariella's birth mother. The way the two of them interacted suggested to me that a special bond existed. And I think it was exactly that – a special bond – a valuable relationship degraded by the emotional warzone existing between Victoria and Penelope. This constant tension between the two people Mariella loved dearly drove her mad, Victoria being the antagonist in Penelope's story and the protagonist in Mariella's.

I never suspected Mariella had buried her anxiety, distress, and grief. Her absence was felt, her presence embraced by everyone. The emails and letters set in motion a runaway train that she thought she'd derailed years earlier. And though she'd remained strong to care for Penelope - who was still institutionalized – Mariella now had to confront her own pain. Rather than face purgatory, she ran.

I could not get over the fact that Mariella despised me because of my profession. If she had not sent letters to explain how she felt, I would've assumed the worst and spiraled out of control. Her expressions of love for me were intense. Everyone knew how much Mariella loved me because she often demonstrated her affection publicly. I was equally passionate for her. I guess every couple faces the ultimate love test at some point in their journey together. As a divorce lawyer, I've witnessed the crushing and at times, unrecoverable blow to self-esteem and self-worth, rendering individuals hopeless when they realize that their love is not enough.

I didn't have a clue what to do about my own marriage. I wanted her back, but nature had set in motion a race that Mariella felt she had to run – and run without me. Every day left us a little further apart. Silence took on the role of the heated conversation, which often occurs before a divorce. When she felt the need to speak, her eyes delivered the message in a language I could not decipher. My beautiful Mariella was gone, leaving a shell behind to remind me of a life that I could not get back.

I assumed that Mariella was going through a phase because of the bad memories. I was wrong. She left one year after receiving the first letter from the first victim of divorce. I was furious and terrified at the same time. How could she? Why would she? My kids? My home? My life? The empty space became my nightmare. I watched children at the playground like a predator, wanting to experience the deep comfort which only a child can offer a parent. My own children, ripped away from my arms with the vacuuming force of a tornado. I thought about kindergarten and first grade. I'd miss it all and there was nothing deadbeat about my responsibilities as a father. I was there to capture and experience the memories, unlike some of my colleagues who lived at the office and in the courtroom.

None of my friends could offer words of wisdom or comfort. My training as an attorney had not equipped me to keep people together during life's challenges, pitfalls, and mishaps. As a result, I caved in. Instead of fighting for my marriage, I buried myself in the area where I excelled – divorce.

All at once, everything and everyone whom I cared for deeply was gone. I talked to myself often, repeatedly saying things like, "Should I have given up my career in order to keep my family? I could've done something! Why is this happening to me? It wasn't supposed to turn out this way. I'm a good man, loving father, and thoughtful husband."

Checking the mailbox became something I despised. Lots of junk mail and bills arrived, but nothing from my dearest Mariella. The phone remained silent. Her friends wouldn't talk. They treated me like a stranger. What had Mariella told them? My home at 2717 Queens Garden Court had become the loneliest place on earth.

I waited and waited and waited. Finally, on Monday, September 16, 1996, I received a large envelope from Mariella's attorney. It had been an entire year. The package provided no residential address. However, it was postmarked by an Atlanta post office.

Inside the envelope was a picture of Emily Rene and Ricardo, an apology letter from Mariella for not contacting me sooner, and divorce paperwork from a law office in Roswell, Georgia. I searched hopelessly for a phone number to contact my children. Furious, I threw the package across the room.

All I could do was cry. No one was around to see me, so this went on for hours. Before I knew it, I'd missed an entire week from work. I corresponded with my secretary by email to let everyone know that I was still alive; however, I was in no shape to properly represent my clients. My partners suggested we go out for drinks to get my mind off of the divorce. I declined. I simply wanted to be left alone.

The anti-Christ showed up a few days later, and I began plotting. Before long, I'd devised the perfect plan to get rid of Mariella. I let him convince me that my plan was justified. Who did she think she was taking away my kids? Fortunately, my heart wasn't buying it. I still loved and missed Mariella.

Wisdom and I became reacquainted after I sat down and put the foolish thoughts to rest. She was gentle, calming, a source of healing and strength. When I heard her voice on the answering machine, I rushed to the receiver.

Katrina and I had been best friends since middle school. I guess you could say she was the pretty girl next door who all the guys wanted to kiss. Since I knew that most guys were up to no good, I became her self-appointed bodyguard. We went everywhere together. We talked about any and everything. She was almost the sister I never had. I say almost because back then I secretly had a crush on Katrina.

Throughout high school, nothing romantic ever happened between us. After graduation, she went to UCLA to study Psychology and earned her PhD in June 1988. Katrina then opened and successfully operated a counseling practice in San Diego. She closed her practice to join Jack Moreno after they married in August 1993, but continued counseling in the evenings and on weekends.

Jack and Katrina moved to his hometown, Alpharetta, Georgia, to open his gastroenterology clinic in 1994. She ran the office while Jack and his medical staff took care of patients. Katrina figured that it would take about six months for Jack to get his business established and then she'd return full-time to her profession as a counselor for teenage mothers. She'd already formed relationships with prominent Atlanta counselors who were ready to employ her expertise.

The relationship between Katrina and me began to change when I married Mariella in December 1987. Mariella didn't like the idea of me having a close relationship with another beautiful woman. So we decided to stay in touch, but the time we'd enjoyed spending together physically would have to end. Both of us were torn, but knew it was necessary if I was to have a quality relationship with Mariella. I saw Katrina a few times a year before she relocated to Alpharetta.

I sensed the concern in Katrina's voice as she said, "Hello, Koda, are you there?" The firm had informed her that I was out of the office handling a family emergency. Normally, Katrina wouldn't have called me at home, out of respect for Mariella, but wanted to make sure I was okay.

She was in town for a training seminar and figured we could have lunch. We hadn't spoken in two years, so she didn't know about Mariella and me separating. I decided to meet Katrina. It was time for me to get on with my life; at least that's what I told myself. Actually, doing it would prove to be the most difficult challenge I have ever faced.

We met at the Yard House in Long Beach. When she arrived, Katrina looked spectacular. Her smile was dazzling. Her attitude confident. Next to Mariella, Katrina had always been the person whose picture alone brought a smile to my face. Too bad that she and I never . . . you know . . . well . . . let's just say . . . Katrina is a very special woman to me.

I stood and waved her over to our table. We embraced and I kissed her on the cheek. The scent of Katrina's perfume sent my imagination on a journey to some place I longed to revisit. I deeply missed the tranquility that I experienced through romance and intimate, unguarded, unprotected, totally-naked conversation.

Katrina and I had been friends now for more than twenty years. We knew each other intimately, but not romantically. I wondered if she'd ever entertained the thought of us being together. If she was open to the idea, I certainly would not pass up the opportunity. But wait a minute . . . we can't . . . she's married . . . to Jack.

The waitress returned for our orders, and I chose the Ginger Crusted Salmon – a generous portion of Norwegian salmon with snow peas and carrots, spicy peanut vinaigrette, and wasabi mashed potatoes topped with fried carrot strings. It was absolutely delicious. Katrina had a taste for something spicy. She ordered the Jerk Chicken with Shrimp Stack – a spiced grilled chicken breast with mango zucchini salsa and shrimp enchilada with jack cheese, corn, pasilla peppers, tomatillo, and red chile sauce.

We spent the entire afternoon laughing, crying, listening to, and consoling one another. To my surprise, her marriage of three years to Jack had also ended. She'd spent the last year looking for her self-esteem and self-confidence.

"Jack Moreno was an insecure control freak," she told me. When Katrina decided to leave the office manager position in his medical office to pursue her passion for helping teenage mothers, Jack became physically and emotionally abusive.

Katrina found strength and guidance through a study group and mind transformation ideology called *A Course In Miracles (ACIM)*. The teaching from *A Course In Miracles (ACIM)* inspired Katrina to love herself. She said, "The course does not aim at teaching the meaning of love, for that is beyond what can be taught. It does aim, however, at removing the blocks to the awareness of love's presence, which is your natural inheritance. Once the blocks were removed, a remarkable strength was cultivated in my heart, allowing me to forgive Jack and then move on to a better choice."

I responded, "Wow," and then told Katrina I wanted to know more about *A Course In Miracles (ACIM)*. She suggested I read <u>A Return To Love</u> by Marianne Williamson. I purchased a copy that evening on my way home from the restaurant.

After showering, I got dressed, picked up Katrina from her hotel, and we went dancing. We concluded the evening with a touch of romance. Making love to her was intoxicating; thoroughly satisfying. Katrina took an extra week's vacation, and we enjoyed each other's company at the romantic La Sultana Hotel in Morocco. She reminded me of the many pleasures a woman brings to a man's life. We spent countless hours on the phone and enjoyed several weekend getaways during the two years which followed. We looked at rings and discussed a future together.

I'm forever grateful to God for sending Katrina to California. After learning and applying *A Course In Miracles (ACIM)*, I developed a love and respect for life, which changed me at the core of my being. In spite of the divorce, finalized February 14, 1997, the changes prompted by *A Course In Miracles (ACIM)* also allowed Mariella and me to rebuild a relationship suitable for raising our children.

After strongly considering a career change, I completed the course for my doctorate in sociology and began devising a five-year plan to build a successful practice in California and then open a second facility in the Atlanta area. My thesis outlined the blueprint for the ultimate counseling center for couples. My new career as a marriage counselor gave me the incomprehensible fulfillment that was missing while serving as an attorney. Instead of legally separating families, today I strategically help put and keep them together. I've preserved my partnership with MBYKT, serving as a consultant to fellow attorneys and counselor to their clients who really want to stay married, but cannot see the possibility of making the pain cease. Our track record is impeccable – seven out of ten couples make the shift and do what's necessary to enjoy their marriage again. I love my new job.

Dr. Takoda Yuma

Chapter 6

Geovana Finds Hope

Reigniting The Passion

Mindow, Branson, Yuma, Klever, and Thesby, LLP
12601 Wilshire Boulevard, Suite 900
Los Angeles, CA 90025
Phone: (310) 447-8657
Fax: (310) 447-8687
www.mbyktlaw.com

Thank you for choosing Mindow, Branson, Yuma, Klever, and Thesby, LLP (MBYKT) to represent you in this important and life-changing decision. Our goal at MBYKT is to help you experience a balanced, fair, and civil marital dissolution. Our professional team will help you rebuild your life, after the case is finalized. We promise to handle your case efficiently, leveraging the applicable laws to ensure you receive a fair share of the combined assets and liabilities.

Please complete this form to begin the process.

Full Name (Husband):	Joshua Fernando Cortez
Full Name (Wife):	Geovana Castaneda Cortez
Number of Children (under 18):	0
Date of Marriage:	10/17/94
Date of Separation:	08/03/99 (Still living together)
Married In Which City and State:	Los Angeles, CA
Is The Wife Currently Pregnant:	Yes (No)

Husband's Employer:	Self-Employed / Real Estate
Husband's Salary:	$100K / month
Wife's Employer:	PCH Properties Realty
Wife's Salary:	$15K / month
Bank Name and Checking Acct #:	Suntrust Bank
Checking Account Balance:	$15K
Bank Name and Savings Acct #:	Bank of America
Savings Account Balance:	$75K
Other Income Source(s):	
Total Income (All Sources):	$90K / I don't have Joshua's

Please list all property that the two of you own together.

No joint property / Everything is in Joshua's name

What arrangement is being made concerning the property?

No arrangements have been made

Is there anything else you would like to include as part of your settlement agreement?

I don't want a long drawn out case. I only want to walk away with no debt and the money from my checking and saving accounts. I also want to keep my vehicle. Joshua can have everything else if he agrees to these terms.

The attorney assured me that I'd likely keep the income in my checking and savings, as well as the vehicle. Oddly, he also required that I see a counselor prior to filing for divorce, a standard practice at their firm.

I couldn't tell my parents. My father would have only made me feel like a fool. He advised not to marry Joshua, but I didn't listen and I've paid dearly.

Joshua's abuse left me hollow and lifeless. I just wanted to be held and have someone tell me that I was beautiful and loved.

I abandoned true love in exchange for Joshua's con game and money. Immaturity and bad advice swayed me to believe that Jackson's conviction equaled a life of continuous struggle, financial insufficiency, and the end of his dream. I wish I could have stood by Jackson. He really needed me and I chose not to be there for him. Even if Jackson agreed to take me back, I knew he deserved better. How could he ever trust me, I thought? I'd committed an unforgivable crime.

Shari didn't know about consultation with the attorney. I wanted to give her a break from my relationship woes. She must have thought I was a complete mess, but always said something to make me feel good about myself. So I picked up the phone and called her because I really needed a boost.

892-7425

Hi Shari, it's Geo. I need your help. Do you have a minute?

Of course I do, girl. What's going on now?

I visited an attorney last week and he requires that I see a counselor before he proceeds with my divorce filing. Can you get in touch with the marriage counselor in Atlanta and get a few names for me? The attorney only provided the name for one counselor and I'd prefer to contact a few before I make my decision.

> I've already called. After our last conversation, I knew it was just a matter of time. My marriage counselor friend introduced me to Katrina Vascuez, who counsels teenage mothers. Katrina spent some time in San Diego before moving to Atlanta and recommends a counselor named Takoda Yuma.

Whoa! The attorney also recommended this person. What else did Katrina say about him?

> Dr. Yuma's is a high profile divorce attorney turned marriage counselor. His program is one of the best in the country. Though a little expensive, he guarantees the results. Dr. Yuma's primary goal is to help you love yourself – something you definitely need right now. Katrina mentioned that he uses the Bible and something called *A Course In Miracles (ACIM)* to assist his patients with the healing process. I've never heard of *A Course In Miracles (ACIM)*, but Katrina says that it's a powerful healing tool. In fact, she uses it to counsel teenage mothers and the results have been astounding.

Bible??? Hmmm! I don't know about that, Shari.

> Just call him. Here's the number: 323-256-9993.

Okay, I'll call. Thanks. Love you!

> I love you too, Geo! I'm here if you need me. Bye!

After speaking with Shari, I felt much better. I contacted Dr. Yuma's office and set up an appointment for the following Thursday. His assistant asked for my email address and forwarded Dr. Yuma's New Patient Orientation to me for review. I marked my calendar and set the reminder.

Subject:	Counseling Session With Dr. Yuma	
Location:		∨

Start Time:	Thu 9/16/1999	∨	2:30 PM	∨	☐ All day event
End Time:	Thu 9/16/1999	∨	3:30 PM	∨	

The New Patient Orientation was impressive. Reviewing the diagram made me think about a passage of scripture my mother used to quote when I was younger: "[2] Dear brothers and sisters, when troubles come your way, consider it an opportunity for great joy. [3] For you know that when your faith is tested, your endurance has a chance to grow. [4] So let it grow, for when your endurance is fully developed, you will be perfect and complete, needing nothing. (James 1:2-4 NLT)

I began to realize that these three verses had something to do with my strength and self-image. I'd spent so much time focusing on what Joshua was not doing, that I'd neglected my own well-being. I knew it was time for a makeover.

Dr. Yuma facilitated ten sixty-minute sessions, over a ten to twenty week period. Some of his clients attended weekly and others bi-weekly. His fee was $6,000 for the ten sessions, and it included a hassle-free money-back guarantee. If he was unable to help you, the first session was free. However, if he decided to work with you, $600 was due at the start of each session.

What I found most interesting was the way each of his nine counseling topics centered on creating a tailor-fitted and enriching marriage. Dr. Yuma explained that everything hinges on clarity. He states, "Most marriages have no destination. They're just together because if feels good; at least in the beginning. When the feeling wears off and you've not chosen a destination for your marriage, the two of you will begin to attack rather than love one another."

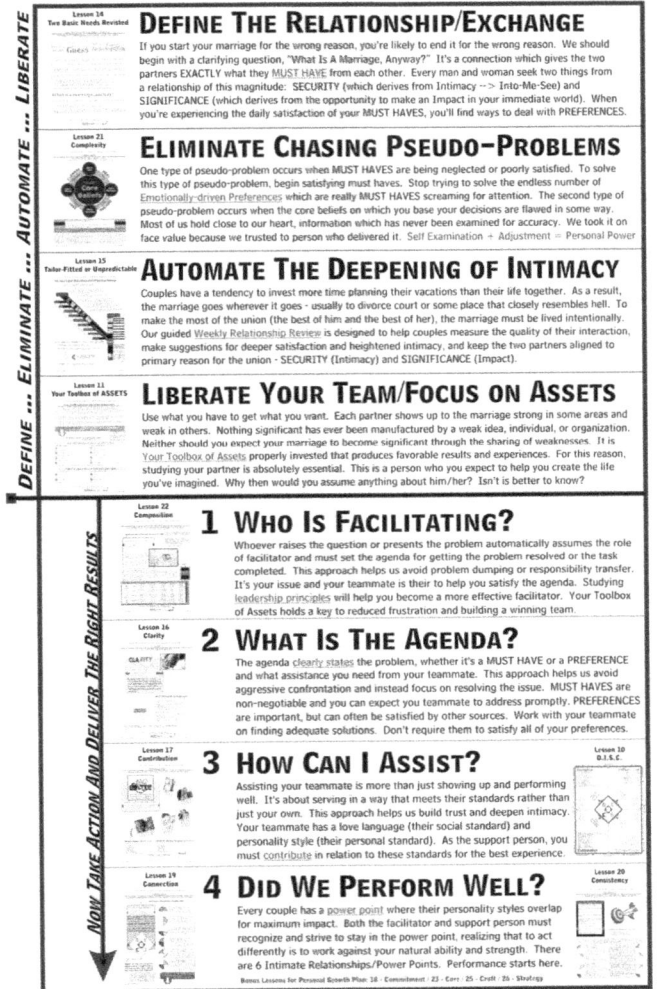

He proposed that experiencing an enjoyable marriage depends on the path you've chosen rather than your intention alone. Intention has a place, but it the chosen path which determines where you'll end up. CLARITY – the first of the 9 Cs of Trust and Intimacy – is where change begins.

I hadn't considered that direction rather intention determines destination. Dr. Yuma's New Patient Orientation reminded me that my life was not over. I only needed to choose a new path; a path leading to the life I wanted to experience.

I also learned an important relationship principle; INTIMACY is about a delightfully irresistible closeness. It is the fusion of two sets of amazingly distinct failures, successes, and dreams. Rather than find someone with the same interests, instead connect with someone on the right path, heading to the right destination - a delightfully irresistible closeness. Intimacy!

My ideal partner is not only someone with great qualities, but also a man traveling a path which leads to a tailor-fitted and enriching marriage. He's someone who supports my dreams, as well as my preferences. He's a man with great vision, communication skills, ambition, self-control, a gentle hand, a sharp mind, and a strong sense of family. He's a man who will allow me to make a significant contribution to his life as wife and partner. He is someone like Jackson.

The final page of Dr. Yuma's Orientation discussed why he used the Bible and *A Course In Miracles (ACIM)* in his counseling program. He used the Bible to help his clients restore confidence and *A Course In Miracles (ACIM)* principles to teach his clients how to forgive. Though I didn't understand how it would happen, I knew intuitively that my life was going to change for the better.

Before attending her first session, Geovana began to consider and journal in detail, how Joshua's sexual appetite had changed her. The beautiful ideas she'd once held about love and intimacy had become distorted and unattractive. She was determined to regain her innocence and redefine herself as a woman worthy of Jackson's love.

Chapter 7

Geovana Comes Alive

Session 1: You're Not Stuck, You Can Choose Again

I arrived at Dr. Yuma's office around 2:00pm to complete the new patient forms. It was nothing like a typical doctor's office. The walls were covered with vibrant colors, pictures of some of the greatest leaders around the globe, and quotations from the most brilliant authors the world has ever known. I was in awe, standing in a place which recognized and highlighted the genius that lies within us all.

The words of Marianne Williamson quickly apprehended my mind; I surrendered without a fight:

> When we were born, we were programmed perfectly. We had a natural tendency to focus on love. Our imaginations were creative and flourishing, and we knew how to use them. We were connected to a world much richer than the one we connect to now, a world full of enchantment and a sense of the miraculous.

What I discovered was just the thing I needed to begin my transformation. I'd been waiting years for the opportunity to taste, smell, and feel what it is like to be free – *free from the prisons of regret, sorrow, and guilt.* That ill-fated evening in May 1989 landed Jackson in prison and me in some place comparable - a place not far from hell. My sentence was until the end of time; at least that's what I thought before meeting Dr. Yuma.

Reading Marianne's words provided relief from much of the pain I'd been enduring for years. I began to picture myself back on that stage, speaking poetically not only to Jackson, but also to all the women who had been deprived of the strength to hold on to true love.

Thinking back on Marianne's words, I was inspired to write these as a healing ointment to our wounded hearts:

Love is what we're born with; fear is what we learned here,

The spiritual journey is a path which intelligently erases the fear.

Acceptance of, this thing called LOVE,

Into my heart, a brand new start.

A beautiful love song, enchantment belongs,

Inside my mind, no longer blind.

Imagination, creatively amazing,

A world much richer is what I now see.

I embrace the beauty, which makes me unique,

God's love for me, gives me the power to believe.

And now . . . I know!

I am a sight to behold!

I completed the forms and returned the clipboard to the receptionist. The positive energy in the office provided a sense of tranquility and warmth that I hadn't experienced since my intimate conversations with Jackson. I felt as though I'd been freed, simply because I showed up with an open mind.

I continued to explore the fascinating components of the facility. As I passed Dr. Yuma's office, a plaque to the left of his door caught my eye. It posed a question about leadership. No author was listed, so I'm not sure who should get credit. The words were penetrating and the question at the end really made me think about the quality of my decisions.

THE 4 TYPES OF LEADERS

The BEST LEADER is indistinguishable from those being led.
He or she educates and empowers the people.

The NEXT BEST LEADER enjoys the love and praise of the people.
He or she serves the people.

The POOR LEADER rules through coercion and fear.
He or she manipulates and exploits the people.

And the WORST LEADER is a tyrant despised by the multitudes.
He or she enslaves and destroys the people.

Which type of leader are you? Would the people whom you've led agree without hesitation? If not, what are you going to do about it?

At 2:30pm, a tall and handsome Dr. Yuma came out of his office to greet me, wearing a blue pin-striped suit, sky blue shirt and matching tie, and blue crocodile-skin shoes. His face was clean-shaven and smooth as a baby's bottom. Our eyes met and he extended his hand to greet me. "Geovana, it is a pleasure to finally meet you. Please come into my office."

He looked into my eyes when he spoke. I felt special. His presence made me feel tender and desirable.

Inside his office, there were no chairs - just three bean bags on the floor. He took my coat and asked me to remove my shoes. The carpet felt good beneath my feet. This whole experience seemed a bit strange, but I went along with the program because it felt good to be there. Then he asked me to lie on my back, with my head on the bean bag. He did the same; our feet faced in opposite directions.

Dr. Yuma referred to this exercise as "The Unity of Minds." He learned this as a boy on the Indian reservation from his father - a great healer and Indian chief. Dr. Yuma believed that people form healthy connections to one another based on what they "think about" the other person, rather than what is true or factual.

The "Unity of Minds" was adapted to limit the projection of negative emotions during the counseling sessions. Dr. Yuma stated, "Facial expressions and cold body language make it difficult for couples to get to the heart of their marital problems. By limiting the projection of negative emotions, I am usually able to persuade the couple to share their thoughts, not only about what they've experienced, but more importantly, about what they'd like to experience. This insight allows me to point out the real problem. Once the couple agrees, I provide specific daily tasks to help them create the type of experiences they want."

He dimmed the lights and the ceiling came to life. What appeared to be a plain white ceiling was a specially designed screen for displaying information being discussed by the doctor and patient. The image on the ceiling displayed a collage of happy couples; everyone was smiling. There were people of different ages and nationalities. Dr. Yuma remained silent while I studied each picture. The next image was a picture of me, lying on the bean bag, happy and sparkling. I stared at the woman on the ceiling, thinking to myself, "This can't be me." I must have given voice to my thoughts because Dr. Yuma replied, "Yes, it is you."

I closed my eyes and held myself tightly. When I opened them, the picture of me still appeared on the ceiling with a slide presentation to the right. The first slide was titled The Secret To Solving Every Problem.

He began advancing the slides and asked me to read aloud. "In most cases, the quality of our relationships is simply a matter of perception. It is a reflection of what we've chosen to see, hear, and feel - the byproduct of our preferences and judgments. The secret to solving every problem is to choose again, not according to where we've been, but in alignment with where we're going. Each step in our journey called life provides us another opportunity to choose again. In most relationships, couples decide not to. The marriage then loses its significance and divorce becomes a topic of interest - the way out of a living hell. My aim, as your counselor, is to restore significance to the institution of marriage and influence you to make your relationship an attractive, fulfilling experience. Today you will learn how to choose again."

Slide 8 presented a passage from the Bible. There was silence as I pondered the last sentence: "First remove the plank from your own eye, and then you will see clearly to remove the speck that is in your brother's eye."

And why do you look at the speck in your brother's eye, but do not perceive the plank in your own eye? Or how can you say to your brother, "Brother, let me remove the speck that is in your eye," when you yourself do not see the plank that is in your own eye? Hypocrite! First remove the plank from your own eye and then you will see clearly to remove the speck that is in your brother's eye.

Luke 6:41-42 (NKJV)

After allowing me time to take it all in, Dr. Yuma broke his silence and we began a dialogue:

Geovana, what would you like to see happen in your marriage?

To be honest, I would like to see it end. I no longer desire to stay with him.

Are you absolutely sure?

Yes, I am. I've been humiliated, ignored, robbed of my innocence, stripped of everything which makes me beautiful and attractive, and now I want it back.

Okay. Are you open to discussing your marriage, so that I can better assist you in getting what you want from our sessions?

Yes. Feel free to ask whatever questions you believe are necessary.

First, I want you to know that God's guidance will ultimately be the source of your healing and restoration. He'll replace your fear and pain with wisdom and comfort. In turn, you will be equipped to make better choices and have the courage to say no to experiences and people who no longer offer any benefit to your life. Whatever the case, learn to ask God what is the best course of action.

And how do you suggest I go about this task of asking God to help me?

The way is simple: Just ask, in whatever way you know how. Once you've asked, try to find or create a quiet place. My experience has revealed that God's answers usually come to us when we've removed all the noise – *people, places, and things, which tend to distract and confuse.* Then, while you're in your quiet place, read the book of James chapter 1 verses 2 through 8. Read it slowly, preferably in the Amplified translation.

> Consider it wholly joyful, my brethren, whenever you are enveloped in or encounter trials of any sort or fall into various temptations. Be assured and understand that the trial and proving of your faith bring out endurance and steadfastness and patience. But let endurance and steadfastness and patience have full play and do a thorough work, so that you may be (people) perfectly and fully developed (with no defects), lacking in nothing.
>
> If any of you is deficient in wisdom, let him ask of the giving God (Who gives) to everyone liberally and ungrudgingly, without reproaching or faultfinding, and it will be given him. Only it must be in faith that he asks with no wavering (no hesitating, no doubting). For the one who wavers (hesitates, doubts) is like the billowing surge out at sea that is blown hither and thither and tossed by the wind. For truly, let not such a person imagine that he will receive anything (he asks for) from the Lord, (For being as he is) a man of two minds (hesitating, dubious, irresolute), (he is) unstable and unreliable and uncertain about everything (he thinks, feels, decides). James 1:2-8 (Amplified Bible)

Wow, Dr. Yuma! I've read this passage of scripture many times in the New Living translation. However, the Amplified translation is new to me. Please tell me more about it.

> The Amplified Bible translation focuses on clarity and understanding. It has provided me a practical, foolproof explanation of Bible scripture without getting too far away from the accuracy I believe is presented in the King James translation. I enjoy studying the King James as well, but I choose not to recommend it to my clients. Its antiquated language oftentimes leaves people confused; at least until their relationship with God matures, and He becomes their primary teacher.

I read about *A Course In Miracles (ACIM)* in the orientation package. How does *A Course In Miracles (ACIM)* fit into the equation?

> *A Course In Miracles (ACIM)* teaches you how to open your mind to the possibility that there may be a better way to accomplish your goals and solve your problems. God in His infinite wisdom understands that our knowledge is limited. He also understands a great deal more about decision-making and the hidden factors which make it difficult for us to plan and act wisely. So, He makes himself available to guide us. God knows we can't get the best results without Him.

> The Bible teaches us in John chapter 15 that *God is the vine, and we are the branches, and if we stay connected to the vine, we will bear much fruit.* And what exactly does He mean by fruit? In the book of Galatians chapter 5 verses 22 and 23, fruit represents the characteristics we'll exhibit as we mature in God's way of cultivating relationship. There are nine fruits, the first being Love. Next are Joy, Peace, Patience, Kindness, Goodness, Faithfulness, Gentleness, and Self-control. Have you ever studied the Fruit of the Spirit?

I've heard of it before, but I've never studied it.

What about the passage of scripture in John chapter 15?

I can honestly say that I've never heard that scripture before, but it certainly makes sense.

True fulfillment is the reward when we (the branches) deliberately choose to stay connected to God (the vine). He won't force us, but He will allow things to happen to us to give us a compelling reason to change our approach and ask for guidance. I want you to know and be fully persuaded that God is here for you, in spite of what you've experienced or done. Also, know that this journey is not about my ability, expertise, charm, or techniques. It is about you allowing God to cleanse and heal you. I am committed to guiding you through the cleansing and healing processes. However, keep in mind that God is running the show. In other words, remain flexible and open to uncommon solutions.

You present these ideas so well. Who taught you about the Bible?

God taught me. Studying *A Course In Miracles (ACIM)* has been the pathway that God uses to instruct and guide me. He cultivates my relationship with Him through *A Course In Miracles (ACIM)*. I believe each person is given a pathway to God which best suits his or her unique set of abilities and circumstances. Once you're healed, I'm positive you will also become a vessel through which God heals others. Our fulfillment comes through our willingness to prepare for and fully engage this special assignment from God. I'm confident that God will send you to heal a group of people who are directly connected to your dreams and talents. How does this idea make you feel?

It makes me feel valuable and significant. It makes me feel happy. It feels like love.

Love is a wonderful thing. In fact, the Bible teaches us that God uses something called PERFECT LOVE to heal and mature us. Perfect love is a gentle love, an enduring love, an intelligent love, a triumphant love, a love we cannot live and do without. Before we continue, would you mind if we looked at God's definition of Love?

No, I don't mind at all.

Great! We're going to look at First Corinthians chapter 13 from a new perspective. Where the author uses the word "Love" we will substitute the word "God." The basis for this substitution is First John chapter 4 verse 8 which teaches us that GOD IS LOVE. We'll read these words together on three – one, two, three:

> God is patient, God is kind. God does not envy, God does not boast, God is not proud. God is not rude, God is not self-seeking, God is not easily angered, God keeps no record of wrongs. God does not delight in evil but rejoices with the truth. God always protects, always trusts, always hopes, always perseveres. God never fails. First Corinthians 13:4-8 (NIV)

Okay, Dr. Yuma. I have a question. If God keeps no record of wrongs, why does the church feel like such a condemning place? It does not seem to me that the people in church are given the freedom to make mistakes or the option of challenging information, which may have been presented in error. My father, a licensed minister, has expected excellence from me in everything. However, he's never given me a reason to want to follow his leadership. Instead of teaching me how to be an excellent student, he punished me when my grades where anything less than "A." Because of his approach, I have despised him most of my life. This brings to mind the quote on leadership I saw posted outside your door. My father is the personification of the poor leader who rules through coercion and fear.

> I understand your frustration, Geovana. Remember, this is about your wholeness, not your father's. To heal completely, your thoughts about your father must mature and evolve. You'll have to learn how to give up your right to be angry and resentful. It will be difficult, but not impossible. The goal is to get what you want, and you've already proven to yourself that anger and resentment offer you nothing but more pain.

But, I don't know how to let go. I lived under his tyrant-like rules for six years. Part of my reason for moving to California and marrying this jerk was to get away from my father. It seems that, in many ways, I married the man I was running away from. Joshua is, in many ways, my father without the religion. He tears me down every time I make a mistake – at least a mistake in his eyes.

> Geovana, what's important today is that you move away from the thoughts that bring you pain. It's been taught by some of our greatest teachers that whatever you give your attention to will grow, whether it is good for you or not. If you want this pain and anger you feel toward your father to end, you must quit feeding it your attention. It's the only permanent solution. Whatever you stop feeding will die, eventually. You have so much to offer. Begin giving your attention to the things that you absolutely love, and I guarantee you'll have more positive and rewarding experiences. Do you agree?

I guess so, since you put it that way. But how do I make this change?

> I'm glad you asked. There are two things you'll want to begin practicing daily. The first is an affirmation of the person you desire to be. Life is a continuous process of growing and changing. Each

day, you should strive to become a little stronger, wiser, and better than you were the previous day. Inch by inch, it's a cinch; But by the yard it's hard. Do you think you can take it one day at a time?

Yes, I can take it one day at a time.

Good! Earlier in the session, we substituted the word "God" in place of love. For your daily affirmation, which you'll read aloud three times a day, substitute "Geovana" in place of love. Please read with me:

Geovana is patient, Geovana is kind. Geovana does not envy, Geovana does not boast, Geovana is not proud. Geovana is not rude, Geovana is not self-seeking, Geovana is not easily angered, Geovana keeps no record of wrongs. Geovana does not delight in evil but rejoices with the truth. Geovana always protects, always trusts, always hopes, always perseveres. With God on her side, Geovana never fails.

First Corinthians 13:4-8 (NIV)

I realize you're not quite there yet. Don't let this fact stop you. The facts stop those who lack the passion and tenacity to go after what they really, really want. According to John Maxwell, "Success is found in your daily routine." To make success almost certain, I suggest that you not only practice daily, but also forecast the future. The Bible teaches us to, "Call those things that be not, as though they were." You'll begin doing specific things daily to develop the skills, acquire the tools, and cultivate the confidence needed to create the exact future experiences you desire. Get it?

Yes! I got it!

The second thing you'll practice daily is found in Luke chapter 6. We covered this at the beginning of our session. Please read aloud slowly, the words that appear on the ceiling. And be careful not to receive them as an insult. Instead, consider these words as you would a great discovery.

And why do you look at the speck in your brother's eye, but do not perceive the plank in your own eye? Or how can you say to your brother, "Brother, let me remove the speck that is in your eye, when you yourself do not see the plank that is in your own eye?" Hypocrite! First remove the plank from your own eye and then you will see clearly to remove the speck that is in your brother's eye.
Luke 6:41-42 (NKJV)

How does this passage of scripture relate to your marriage, Geovana?

Well, I have spent most of my time thinking about what my husband has done. *Whoa! I've been completely distracted by the things I enjoy least.* Based on what you've shared with me, I now realize that I've been my worst enemy. I have deliberately chosen to hold on to the things I don't want.

Exactly! I have discovered through counseling many couples that the real problem is the inability to extend compassion or forgiveness. Through forgiveness, reconciliation and restoration are made possible. First, you must become open to the possibility that there's a better way to live life and navigate through life's challenges. Do you agree?

You may have a point. Please tell me more.

A Course In Miracles (ACIM) teaches us that we (the branches) think we have many problems, but we only have one — *our seeming separation from God (the vine).* Fulfillment comes through staying connected to the vine, not by fighting with or trying to prove wrong the other branches. Your husband is a branch on the tree, just like you. So is your father. Neither is the source of life nor fruitfulness; they are not a pathway to your fulfillment. It is God's responsibility to lead us to fulfillment, and fulfillment begins with receiving love – the God kind of love. Then, through relationship with others, we are given the opportunity to share the abundance of what God has given us. Love is the ultimate tool for healing and restoration.

So basically, you're saying that God is the answer to all of my problems?

Yes.

Well, I don't agree with that. Many times, I have gotten down on my knees and prayed to God for hours, and He's answered none of my prayers. How do you know that the Bible and *A Course In Miracles (ACIM)* present the true words of God?

Geovana, it's not about the words, but the results you experience when applying the words. I evaluate spiritual doctrine by its ability to help me produce results. I intend to equip you with the skills to solve problems, God's way. From what you've shared with me, you have not been properly educated about the things and ways of God. However, that's OK.

When you leave here today, I know with absolute certainty, you will become the person we've discussed, and you won't need me or anyone else to validate you. You'll be able to stand on your own - confident, wise, and fascinatingly attractive to all who observe. The world is waiting for you to evolve; eagerly anticipating your rise. And know this: Your evolution is a cooperative effort between you, God, and the teachers you'll meet along the way. During the cleansing process, God usually presents lessons to help you make sense of your past experiences. This allows you to have a healthy relationship with your past, rather than one which gives birth to guilt, indifference, blame, or regret. When He is finished laying the new foundation in your heart and mind, you'll appreciate all you've had to endure. Your pain and suffering will not have been in vain.

Okay, Dr. Yuma! I'll do it.

Great! You've made a wonderful decision. Are you satisfied with our first session?

Yes.

I'm excited and thank you for this opportunity. Please make an appointment with the receptionist and settle today's fee. In session two, we'll discuss compassion and companionship. I'll see you in two weeks.

Chapter 8

Dr. Yuma Was Right

Session 2: Compassion and Companionship

Geovana left Dr. Yuma's office and headed straight to the airport. She was excited about the ten-night South Pacific cruise she'd planned with Shari, who had landed thirty minutes earlier. Geovana boarded the plane, bound for Sydney, Australia. Seeing Shari was like a warm blanket on a cold winter morning. They hugged and took their seats. She told Shari about her session with Dr. Yuma and thanked her for the recommendation.

In Sydney, they spent two days indulging the city's foods, sights, and sounds. They even decided to get tattoos. Sharing these experiences with her best friend solidified the confidence which Dr. Yuma had imparted. On the third day, they boarded the Royal Caribbean cruise ship and set sail.

The daily affirmation and Bible study rewarded Geovana immeasurably. Between shows, excursions, and on-board activities, she spent time reading and relaxing by the pool. Geovana exited the ship refreshed, rejuvenated, and ready to rebuild her life. Upon returning home, she checked her email and had a message from Dr. Yuma's assistant. The message confirmed her next appointment and invited her to come out to see Marianne Williamson discuss applying *A Course In Miracles (ACIM)*. Shari joined her for the counseling session and seminar.

When I arrived for my second session, I relived the initial experience all over again. It was just as fascinating. However, this time we didn't go into the room with the bean bags.

We walked down the hall and entered the Imagination and Discovery Room. Its atmosphere was emancipating – free from restrictions, rules, and limits. The wall directly across from the glass door framed a huge window which overlooked a beautiful rose garden. Tools used to express creativity clothed the walls. A montage of great inventors decorated the ceiling, along with quotes from Thomas Edison. In one quote, Mr. Edison suggested, "What you are, will show in what you do." I thought to myself, I would have written, "*Who* you are, will show in what you do."

Dr. Yuma kindly asked Shari and me to have a seat. The recliner hugged my body perfectly. Once he knew we were comfortable, Dr. Yuma took his seat, across from me this time. The recliners were arranged, as if to form a triangle. I leaned forward and reached for their hands, smiling as I thanked them for listening to and supporting me.

Then I noticed the music playing. The piano solo filled the space with an abundant presence of power. I felt God's touch and stood to my feet. It was a quiet celebration, though inside, I could see myself laughing and cheering enthusiastically. All the while, Dr. Yuma and Shari remained in their seats, expressing no desire to interrupt the unfolding.

I walked over to the window to view the rose garden. Reds and yellows and pinks and whites sun bathing. Dr. Yuma observed intently. He studied my expressions and movement. He connected to my experience. I felt safe and confident. When I returned to my recliner, I initiated the conversation.

Dr. Yuma, where did you get the idea for the design of this beautiful office?

> From the same source that will help facilitate your dreams. The Bible teaches us in the book of James chapter 1 verse 17, "Every good and perfect gift is from above." God is the source of extraordinary ideas, as well as the Master Architect. His specialty is the reconstruction of man and woman, especially husband and

wife. Before we continue, have you considered our discussion from session one?

Yes I have.

And what did you take from it?

Most of all, I realize what I desire for my life will require me to change my focus and develop patience. Rather than give time and energy to the problem as I perceive it, instead I should invest in my relationship with God. The return I can expect to receive from this investment is the wisdom required to guarantee my success.

Excellent! In the book of Joshua chapter 1 verse 8, the Bible teaches us to study God's ways, standards, practices, and love. For, in this pursuit, we discover the blueprint which will make our lives prosperous and successful. Are you ready for today's lesson?

Yes, I've been looking forward to meeting again. And thank you for the invitation to Marianne's presentation. I can't wait to see her. I read her book last week while we were cruising with Royal Caribbean. The content was engaging and I thoroughly enjoyed reading her words. She handles the difficult issues of life with great passion and responsibility. Her words are gentle and soothing, offering the gift of change, as would a caring and determined mother, someone whom you can trust and turn to for encouragement and direction.

May I ask, which book did you read?

A Return To Love.

Perfect! Today's session will center on the need to extend compassion, not only to others, but also to ourselves. Marianne's book covered this concept in depth. Here's what I hope you learn about compassion: *God fills us with love, so that we can give love to those who have lost it, or quite possibly never received it.* People behave in relation to what they think they know. The problem is most people don't know how to think; they simply have not developed good thinking skills. And it's not their fault. Memorization is emphasized in most schools. Good thinking and careful analysis are not. As a result, we've produced children who make the same relationship mistakes as their parents.

Good point, but how do we correct it?

I think it starts with people like you and me. For instance, as a communicator, you hold a key to helping others see more clearly the results they've produced. The most powerful form of communication is not verbal or written, but a helping hand. When you show up ready to help, with no hidden agenda, a person's assumptions are respectfully challenged and their deeply rooted fear can be dismantled. Fear has a choke-hold grip on most of us, delaying the arrival of *quality change* in our lives. I have an acronym for the word C.H.A.N.G.E. hanging above my bed. It means **C**ourageously **H**ang-on to **A**nother's **N**atural **G**ifts and **E**xperiences. People need to be led, not only by a commanding voice, but also by a skilled and gentle hand. People want you to walk with them and become intimate with their pain and suffering, setbacks and challenges, with their goals and aspirations. They want you to take the time to build a relationship - *the most suitable platform for the exchange of ideas.*

Relationships provide us the opportunity to know others intimately. Intimacy of this kind is not of a sexual nature; rather it is a cultivated closeness, an undeniable trust, and a true friendship. Marriage, in particular, demands this kind of intimacy. Yet, we fail miserably at meeting this demand because the art of cultivating true friendship has not been emphasized within the institutions which shape and mold the human mind. I'm here to change this reality, one couple at a time, so that our children can have meaningful and lasting relationships. Are you still with me?

Yes!

People who remain at odds, mostly because of their fears and preferences, can never practice and experience intimacy. Without intimacy, there can be no teamwork. Without teamwork, we are left alone to navigate our way through life - the state of most marriages in America. What most couples define as intimacy is really just sex. To prove my point, what generally happens when a couple is facing a difficult relationship problem?

They either start arguing about the stupidest things or ignore each other altogether. Sex is the next thing to go. And if the sex does continue, there's no affection.

Exactly! The absence of true intimacy leaves a big fat wedge in the relationship. And the wedge doesn't go away when they resume having sex. To fix this problem, I believe marriages must be reconstructed on the principles governing true friendship – which are *compassion and companionship*. That is, walk with me, through the fire if you must, so that you may KNOW me and ENCOURAGE me to be all that I am. Sometimes, the circumstances of life can place a layer of dullness over a person's shine. Then a friend comes along to not only remind them about their brilliance, but also to help them get their shine back. This is compassion. This is companionship.

Interesting! Hmmm!

Is there something you want to share?

Oh, No! I'm sorry. Pardon the interruption. Please continue.

No problem. I've learned the reason people do not extend compassion is because they've never received it. You cannot give to others what you do not have for yourself.

Whoa! May I say something now?

Sure.

For several months, I have been beating myself up. Before contacting your office, my self-worth account was overdrawn. Now I realize that I am a divine expression of God. However, the quality of this expression depends upon my relationship with Him and my willingness to allow Him to reshape my thoughts.

Yes! To make this shift, we must let go of the thoughts which create confusion and misunderstanding. The Bible teaches that God is not the author of confusion, but of peace. I learned from my good friend Psoloman Blacksmith that the Bible is written in such a way that every scripture can be validated by other scriptures. He taught me a sure method to make sense of the Bible. I think it's a process you will appreciate. Would you like me to share it with you?

Is it complicated?

No, it's quite simple.

Okay! Let's hear it.

There are five questions you should ask when seeking the Bible for an answer.

1: CLARIFY - What specific problem do I want to solve?
2: STUDY - What does the Bible say about this problem?
3: UNDERSTAND - How does it relate to my experience?
4: DECIDE - What does the Bible require me to do?
5: EXECUTE – When will I start?

The third question is usually the most challenging. A good study Bible and dictionary are invaluable tools when it comes to understanding and applying scripture. The NLT Life Application

Study Bible is an excellent resource. You can request a free copy at the Resource Center before you leave today. It contains everything you will need at this stage. Can you see the importance of asking these questions?

Yes, I think so. May I explain?

Certainly!

Based on what you've shared, doing things God's way is not a mystery. Once I learn to apply the system you've described, solving problems will become much easier. The Bible contains specific instructions on how to experience God's best. Do I understand this properly?

Yes! Yes! Yes! The single word equivalent for experiencing God's best is fulfillment – *a byproduct of God's love and wisdom operating in and through us.* In the book of Jeremiah chapter 29 verse 11, God promises us fulfillment. He says, "For I know the plans I have for you, plans to prosper you and not to harm you, plans to give you hope and a future."

What you're saying is that God offers me fulfillment through my passion for communication?

You've got it! Now that you have a practical system for understanding and applying scripture, the next step is to ask God to show you the best way to use your communication gift. Your daily affirmation and Bible study should help in this area. Become comfortable asking God for guidance in every decision, even the small stuff. It's easy to get stuck in an unfruitful pattern of thinking when it comes to addressing problems. Spending quality time with God will equip you to identify and apply the right solution.

That's refreshing. Tell me something, do you think God will support my desire to reconnect with Jackson?

Who is Jackson? Don't you mean Joshua?

I'm sorry. I thought I mentioned him already. Jackson is my first love.

What happened between you and Jackson?

It's a long story, but basically he went to jail in my defense. There was a sting operation taking place at the nightclub where I was performing. It was Jackson's eighteenth birthday, and I'd delivered a special poem to him. After my performance, I went to the ladies room to freshen up. While waiting in line, a female undercover officer stormed the room, demanding that everyone exit to be frisked for drugs. The undercover male officer placed his hands underneath my dress and touched me. I cursed him and screamed; Jackson came running. He beat the male officer to near death and was convicted as a result.

I tried to stick with him through the five year sentence, but the pressure from my father was too much to bear. After one year of visiting Jackson in prison, I ended our relationship. To this day, the guilt I feel is emotionally exhausting.

Shari is Jackson's cousin. She's been trying to convince me that he wants me back in his life, but I don't have the courage to face him. What I want more than anything from these sessions is the confidence to call Jackson and apologize for leaving him when he needed me most. A friendship with him is sufficient for now.

OK. That's exactly what I'll help you do. We'll customize the program to help you replace your guilt with courage and insight. I'm certain the guilt you feel will not go away until you have a conversation with Jackson. You need to hear his side of the story. However, I would not recommend contacting Jackson until you have worked things out with Joshua. Are you still planning to end the relationship?

Yes! Joshua is history. I've already started looking for a place of my own. I'll need about six months to finalize my business affairs, before moving back to Atlanta. If there's a chance for Jackson and me, I want to give him the very best I have to offer. I have a lot of work to do, but I am committed to doing what is necessary. Since Joshua and I do not have any children, I'm prepared to give up my ownership to our joint assets.

You seem determined to reconnect with Jackson. I promise that I will not try to change your mind. However, I will make you aware of the challenges which lie ahead. And yes, I do believe God will support your desire to reconnect with Jackson. Spend some time talking with God about what you want, so that He can prepare you. Since we're talking about God restoring a previous relationship, what do you think is God's intention for bringing man and woman together?

To create family and express love. Companionship, as you've shared today.

Are you open to a different perspective?

Sure.

God created man and woman as a physical extension of Himself. He created us to become masters at loving others in a physical, tangible way. He gave man and woman very specific roles to play in the process. Man builds and protects; a woman nurtures and comforts. Just as the sun and the earth align to produce food to nourish our bodies, man and woman are designed to work together to exemplify a love which nourishes our minds and transforms our thoughts. However, as brilliant and magnificent as the sun is, as beautiful and phenomenal as the earth is, neither can choose the role it plays in this thing we call life. Man and woman are the only creation to whom God extended the power to choose, and He encourages us to choose Him. He wants us to reflect His power, wisdom, and love. Does this make sense to you?

It does.

We must decide to participate in God's perfect system. The benefits are tremendous. However, while His system is perfect, it is not without adversity. The earth will continue to have tornados, hurricanes, and earthquakes, just as you and I will continue to become angry, say mean things, and hurt others along our path to maturity. The key is to stay on the path, for it is the place of growth and change. Got it?

I got it!

Do you have anything you'd like to add before we end our second session?

Yes. Thank you for opening my eyes to the wonderful things God has in store for me and the tremendous wisdom the Bible contains. I never would have known, based on the experiences I've had with people, that the Bible is a rich source of wisdom and guidance. I realize I have some work to do not only on my thoughts about marriage, but also on the prejudices I've cultivated over the years. If I truly intend to help women communicate effectively, it must begin with me. Thanks again, Dr. Yuma. I look forward to our next session.

After the seminar, Geovana and Shari talked about Jackson. Both shed tears. Geovana was afraid. Shari just loved on her and told her everything was going to be alright. They had an amazing time at Marianne's seminar. Shari purchased a copy of <u>A Return To Love</u> to become acquainted with

Marianne's teachings. She flew back to Atlanta the following morning, confident about Jackson and Geovana's future.

Shari Campbell

Chapter 9

Geovana's Apology

Reconnecting With The Man She Loves

Jackson Gray

From:	GeoThePoet@yahoo.com
Sent:	Sunday, September 19, 1999 7:17 PM
To:	JacksonDGray@yahoo.com
Subject:	My Deepest Apology
Attachments:	Geovana (June99).jpg

Hello JD,

I have cried many nights thinking about how to say this to you. Because of the pain and guilt I feel for leaving you in that terrible place, I have not been able to face you, at least to apologize.

While this is not intended to be a romantic letter, I want you to know that I've never stopped loving you. If you'll forgive me for what I've done, I'd like the opportunity to prove that I can be a good friend.

As you know, I'm married now and things have not gone well in this relationship. I'm currently working on me - getting myself together. This marriage has changed me in ways that I'm not proud of and I hope that my counseling sessions will put me back on track.

I've already filed for divorce, but it's contingent on me completing my counseling sessions. I wish I could have waited for you. I smile when I think about our lofty goals and aspirations as teenagers.

I hope you'll accept my apology.

My Deepest Apology

Leaves wither and die . . .

But they always come back in the springtime

To go back in time and change my decision

I'd do it in a heartbeat to prevent our division

The last nine years would have been spent in your arms

Writing you poetry and keeping you warm

A day has not passed without me envisioning your face

Your smile, your support for me, our special place

I'm sorry for leaving, for no longer believing

Nine years I've been grieving as if we had died

Today we shall rise

Thank you for keeping me inspired

For making me feel desired

For loving me . . . entirely

You mean the world to me

Love, Geovana

Chapter 10

Jackson's Reply and Letter

Does He Truly Want Geovana Back In His Life?

Geovana Cortez

From: JacksonDGray@yahoo.com

Sent: Sunday, September 19, 1999 11:15 PM

To: GeoThePoet@yahoo.com

Subject: Re: My Deepest Apology

Attachment: Letter To Geovana.doc

Geovana,

It was such a delight to open my email and see a message from you. I have longed and prayed for this moment. About a year ago, I wrote you a letter, but felt it was inappropriate to send, given your situation. The letter expresses everything I want you to know.

JD

The first two years without you nearly destroyed me. However, I soon realized that I could no longer allow my prison sentence to negatively impact your life and your dreams.

My decision to protect you was then, and still is today, an honor. I know that I acted selfishly, but I was deeply hurt by what took place. I felt completely violated and, therefore, justified in my actions - actions that eventually led to our separation.

I wish that I could have swallowed my pride, absorbed the hurt and brushed off the humiliation. But the look on your face . . . I mean . . . I just couldn't let him get away with it. The officer should have been charged with statutory rape. Instead, they found a way to place all eyes and blame on me.

I never stood a chance with that jury and defense team. But you know what? Protecting your dignity and self-respect was worth every minute I spent incarcerated. Had we been more mature, maybe our relationship would not have ended. However, life isn't over yet, and we still have time to rebuild something phenomenal.

I apologize for leaving you alone. I'm sorry about the life you've had to experience with Joshua. Please do not be angry with Shari. She knows that you and I should be together and has kept me informed about most things over the years. Some of the things she said infuriated me, but now I'm much better at handling my anger.

In prison, I learned how to channel my anger in a productive and purposeful way. My mentor and good friend, Mr. Clyde Richardson, taught me the value of making quality decisions while under pressure. Mr. Richardson equated prison life with the process of turning coal into diamonds - a process he referred to as The Malcolm X Effect. When you've properly invested your time and skillfully navigated through the prison environment, you have the potential to emerge from prison a diamond - transformed, attractive, and valuable.

In essence, I learned how to convert the prison environment into the equivalent of an Ivy League University. Mr. Richardson used its rigid rules, concrete walls, crooked guards, steel bars, and unbreakable chains, plus a heavy dose of law and economics, to cultivate in me great wisdom, penetrating influence, and immeasurable patience.

Mr. Richardson has been the father I've never had. If only I had known my father, I probably would not have grown up so angry. I was barely a year old when he died. My mother told me all about him in a letter that she wrote to me while I was in prison. She told me that he was a fine detective with the Atlanta Police Department, whom she had dated since high school. His name was Spencer Dwayne Gray.

The picture my mother sent with the letter revealed many similarities between my father and me. He was bi-racial, so his complexion was different. She described him as an articulate speaker, compassionate friend, and deep thinker, who could become violent at times, especially after he'd been drinking.

Although he never struck her, she was forever mindful of his violent temper. She said that I inherited all of his brilliance and about fifty percent of his temperament.

Mom also shared that my father cheated on her with a local politician, shortly before his death. Although

Mom was hurt, she reluctantly took him back. She confronted the other woman and told her, "Stay away from him." Mom said she cried for days before speaking to my father again.

She told me she looked him in the eyes and said, "What really makes me angry and disgusted is your lack of discretion and self-control. You gave my treasured love to a white woman. The crime you've committed exceeds that of the most despicable inmate. There's no sentence proportionate to the responsibility your action has placed upon my heart. I forgive you, but my pain is forever."

As a teenager, Mom was ridiculed and humiliated because she was darker than the other blacks. These experiences caused her to secretly wish that she were white, or at least a lighter shade of black. Today, she acknowledges that her dark skin is beautiful.

When Mom met the other woman (who she refers to as Nikki), she quickly realized what attracted my father to her. Nikki's beauty and complexion were absolutely stunning. In addition to her physical attributes, Nikki's power and influence throughout Dekalb County and much of Georgia was far-reaching and deeply penetrating. Her professionalism and skill with people earned her matchless respect from her colleagues and supporters. Dad's connection to Nikki meant access to greater opportunity. However, his obsession with advancement began to cloud his judgment.

My father and Nikki never intended to become involved romantically, and she was by no means a "loose" woman. The amount of time they spent together professionally created an atmosphere for them to explore their sexual urges and curiosity. After resisting the urge for several months, they finally gave in to the temptation.

Although they only had sex once, Nikki discovered that she was pregnant with his child. This seemingly harmless encounter presented two major problems.

Since Nikki was a strong supporter of Pro-Life - a term that gained popularity a year later with the Roe vs. Wade case - an abortion was out of the question. Roe vs. Wade reshaped national politics and became the fuel that Nikki used to promote her campaign.

Secondly, Nikki knew how difficult it was to grow up in America as a black male child. She had a decision to make - a very difficult decision. The chance of her child having dark skin was slim due to my father's light complexion. If Nikki could somehow get her husband to believe that this was his child, her problem would be solved. My father did not agree with Nikki's decision, but knew that it was in his best interest to retreat. Exposing this secret would have been damaging to her career and could have jeopardized my father's life.

My father didn't receive the promotion he was seeking and began drinking more frequently. The circumstances of the whole ordeal created insurmountable tension between him and my mother. Four months later, he was shot and killed during a drug bust. Mom believes he was murdered by The System. She doesn't blame Nikki exclusively, but she suspects that someone in her inner circle organized the plan for his murder. I guess we'll never know what really happened.

In spite of her suspicions, my mother has maintained a relationship with Nikki over the years. Initially, Nikki tried to pay Mom off to keep her quiet about the sexual encounter. But Mom is from the old school and could not be bought. She simply requested a proper burial from the police department for my father and financial payment due from his insurance policy.

When I asked for the other woman's real name, Mom told me to be patient. She said that when the time is right, I would meet my younger brother. Based on her description of him, he looks white and has lived his life under this pretense. His birth certificate identifies Nikki's husband as the father. Could you imagine having to explain and justify this lie?

What's good to know is that I have a younger brother and, in spite of the circumstances which produced him, I look forward to meeting him someday soon.

While in prison, I learned the importance of family and unity through my Five Percent Nation of Islam brothers. I wonder what they would say if I told them I have a brother who is white. That would be an interesting conversation!

Since leaving prison, my studies have led me to a greater understanding of black and white. I have adopted a theory which supports the idea that racism is nothing more than a scapegoat, created by the powers-that-be to mask the real problem, which I believe is systematic economic oppression. This system flourishes by keeping the majority of people financially illiterate.

I intend to impact the lives of middle-income families by teaching them how to run their homes like successful businesses. I've seen outstanding results during the last year using a board game called Cashflow 101. This game was created in 1996 by Robert Kiyosaki, whose mission in life is similar to my own. I've made some modifications to the game to incorporate "real life" scenarios.

Please excuse me for sharing so much at one time. I remember having conversations with you during our high school years. We would talk about our dreams for hours. I have so much I want to tell you. I hope you'll be patient!

During one of our last conversations before my release, Mr. Richardson asked me, "Do you believe it was your destiny to meet me?" I said to him, after carefully considering the question, "Destiny no, circumstantially yes! Our meeting was simply an opportunity for change. I was given a choice between following you or self-destructing. I chose you because I saw the opportunity to move to a higher level of understanding and make this time in prison more profitable. This decision allowed both of us to rise. You became my father and teacher; I became your son and student. I believe God took a bad situation and turned it around for both of us. God used our shared passion for economics to bring us together." He smiled and then said, "That's how I figured you'd answer."

I miss the time he and I shared, and I pray every day for his freedom. He's been incarcerated since July 1980, almost 20 years. Mr. Richardson told me he received a frantic call and rushed home. When the ordeal was over, a white male police officer lay dead on his living room floor.

When authorities arrived on the scene, Mrs. Richardson was in the corner of the room, eyes swollen, half-naked, and curled in the fetal position. Mr. Richardson knew then, he was on his way to jail.

Although Mr. Richardson may die in prison, he's confident that his dreams will live through my efforts. I promised him I'd do two things -- continue his work in economics and find you to rekindle our love. Though working on this project has greatly challenged me, it hardly compares to the emotional incarceration I experienced, knowing you were with someone else.

Mr. Richardson created an amazing wealth-building program for middle-income families called The Wealth Creation Ladder. During the last three and a half years of my sentence, Mr. Richardson taught me everything. Our book titled <u>My Money Works For Me</u> will be ready to publish in twelve to fourteen months.

Mr. Richardson also inspired me to keep you close to my heart. He encouraged me to hold on to the love I have for you. We talked often about a man's love for a woman. I asked him how his wife could hang on for so long, knowing he'd never be free, to walk with her through the park. He smiled and responded, "She's here every week. It's extremely difficult, but I stay strong because I know she loves me. That's all I need to get by."

Years ago, Mr. Richardson suggested to his wife that they divorce, but she wasn't interested. Every letter that she mailed, after that conversation, closed with the words, "Until death do us part." I want us to develop this kind of love.

I still have your poem "Masculine Virginity." In spite of the pain I've experienced since our separation, the poem reminds me of the times that we smiled, laughed, and enjoyed each other's company. It's framed and hanging on the wall above my bed. I keep it there believing that one day you'll wake up in my arms.

Masculine, his voice deep like the ocean floor,
Always ready to give me more!
Satisfaction . . .
When expressing his love my man is never lacking!
In a physical throw down,
He can take me the full twelve rounds!
Making love to mind,
Oh . . . you thought I was talking about from behind!
Well he's got that too, but this poem is not about the P-U . . .
But the connection,
The bridge between our minds an erection,
His masculinity, it is perfection!
Never does he give me reason to wonder,
About another woman coming to steal my thunder.
Penetration,
The honey comb of my mind is his destination!
His words . . . they massage my ears,
I say to him . . . slow and easy my dear,
I'm not going anywhere.
Do you think I'd give up this moment in time?
To settle for a silver dime,
When you're a silver dollar,
To the end of this life it is you that I follow.
So come here to mama!

Are these words still alive in your heart? Are you willing to follow me to the end of this life? I know that Joshua was simply your means of coping with the pain of our separation and the pressure from your father.

I'm here to comfort you through your divorce and healing. As your friend, as your brother, and soon-to-be life partner, I reach out to touch the part of you who expresses herself poetically. Your poetry has kept me inspired and hopeful during the last nine years. Geovana, my love for you is permanent. JD

Chapter 11

Geovana Risks It All

Changing The Rules Of The Game

Jackson Gray

From:	GeoThePoet@yahoo.com
Sent:	Monday, September 20, 1999 7:52 AM
To:	JacksonDGray@yahoo.com
Subject:	Thank You So Much

JD,

You amaze me. You've grown so much in the last nine years. I want to continue communicating with you, but not like this. Do you mind if I call? I want to hear your voice. I remember how your voice soothed my mind, calmed my fears, and excited my heart.

Tonight I have a project to complete, so it will have to be tomorrow or Wednesday. Send me your number and the best time to call. I will do my best to contain the excitement I feel inside. Thank you for forgiving me. You just don't know how much I appreciate you.

Love,

Geovana

Chapter 12

Jackson's Excitement

The Sweetest Sound In The World

Geovana Cortez

From:	JacksonDGray@yahoo.com
Sent:	Monday, September 20, 1999 10:19 AM
To:	GeoThePoet@yahoo.com
Subject:	Re: Thank You So Much

Good Morning Geovana,

I hope you rested well last night. You must have gotten up early to read the lengthy letter I sent you. I have missed you for so long that I had to tell you everything. Hearing your sweet voice again would definitely be nice.

I have a writer's conference scheduled all day Tuesday in New York. I'll be flying out this evening and will not return until Wednesday afternoon around 3pm. Let's talk Wednesday evening at 6:30pm your time. My cell number is 404-532-7950. I'll be thinking of you. Have a wonderful day.

Love,

JD

Chapter 13

Geovana Is In Heaven

Life Is Starting To Look Wonderful Again

Jackson Gray

From:	GeoThePoet@yahoo.com
Sent:	Monday, September 20, 1999 1:06 PM
To:	JacksonDGray@yahoo.com
Subject:	Re: Thank You So Much

Hi Baby,

6:30pm is perfect. Have a safe trip and wonderful time at the writer's conference. I can't wait to hear about your experience in New York. Well, I have to get back to work. Talk to you on Wednesday.

Just in case you have a minute between sessions, here's my cell number. No pressure. Miss you like crazy!

Love,

Geovana

323-256-9541

Chapter 14

The Fantasy Room

Joshua Forgets His Keys

Joshua woke up late, an unusual occurrence. If he hurried, there was still time to make the flight to Dallas. Fifteen minutes later, the white lights on the back of his Mercedes illuminated.

He didn't say good morning, goodbye, I love you, I can't stand you; he simply looked at her with disgust as he headed to the garage. Used to Joshua's childish behavior, Geovana turned her attention to San Francisco. She planned to meet two eager buyers that afternoon and then attend what promised to be an unforgettable dinner party, hosted by her employer and the company's partners in the bay area.

Geovana finished loading her things into the vehicle and sat down for a lite breakfast – mixed berries over vanilla yogurt. She also brewed a cup of French Roast Eight O'Clock Coffee for the road.

As she reached for the keypad to arm the security system, Geovana noticed the large envelope marked **CONFIDENTIAL - Dallas**. Next to it lay Joshua's cell phone and keys. She reached into her purse. Joshua's assistant answered and they agreed to meet at the base of the canyon.

Since it would take at least twenty minutes for Cassandra to arrive, Geovana had thirteen minutes to see what Joshua was hiding in the fantasy room. The red key did the trick, revealing an exquisite collection of manly possessions, items you'd encounter in The Robb Report. The most striking décor in his man cave, framed by mahogany wood and solid gold trim was her – Geovana. Delicate, sophisticated, refined, adorable, Joshua on bended knee extended a promise to his fascination. The image provoked undeniable indignation. She chuckled to lessen the intensity, ninety-nine degrees and rising. Geovana slammed the door, grabbed Joshua's stuff, and drove off, forgetting to set the alarm. She quickly regained focus, navigating her way down the canyon.   The tight curves and narrow road demanded conformance.

When she reached the PCH, Cassandra embraced her and said, "Lunch, next week?"   Geovana smiled in agreement, knowing she'd find a reason to cancel.

Cassandra phoned Joshua and said, "I'm heading up now. I'll get everything setup. Can't wait until this is over." Joshua responded, "Yes, I know what you mean. See you in Dallas."

Submerged in sinister, Joshua recounted the email messages from Jackson. "My love for you is permanent" filled his veins with poison, his mind with murder.

Chapter 15

The Meeting In Dallas

Expanding The Business and Tripling Profits

Is everything clear on the plan we discussed last night? Proper execution of this plan will expand the operation and triple profits in a year. Don't screw this up or heads will roll. I'm counting on the two of you to make this happen. The package should arrive on Wednesday around 6:00pm. Be there to sign for it.

Click!

Fifty thousand a month in revenue waited for Joshua in Dallas. Cassandra stopped by Fedex to overnight the project to the duplication house for manufacturing and packaging. Joshua continued to marinate in his hatred for Jackson.

Chapter 16

Simply Irresistible

The Importance of Not Deviating From The Plan

At 4:30 on Wednesday afternoon, Joshua's business partners arrived at his Malibu office. They went inside and waited for the package to arrive.

Geovana pulled into the driveway of her million dollar home around 5:30pm. Her trip to San Francisco was quite profitable – a twenty-five thousand dollar commission and five hot prospects. She entered the house, disarmed the security system, and retrieved the red key from her purse. Geovana headed straight to the fantasy room. After opening the door, she was attacked from behind and the door slammed shut. No one could hear her scream.

She begged for mercy. "Take anything," she said, ninety seconds shy of a panic attack. Frankie responded, "Shut up, bitch!" and struck her across her left eye. It closed quickly, swelling to the size of a baseball. She lost her feet and collided with the bed post on her way to the floor.

Alonzo left the room to carry out the next step in the plan. When he was out of sight, Frankie lifted Geovana from the floor and laid her across the edge of the bed. He grabbed her panties on either side. Seconds later, he penetrated her unconscious body, talking to her as if they were secret lovers having rough sex.

Alonzo re-entered the room. Frankie climaxed. Alonzo yelled, "What the hell are you doing?" and tackled him. "Have you lost your damn mind? This is not part of the plan. That crazy bastard is going to kill both of us."

They struggled with each other for a moment and then headed for the basement to get the laptop and exit the house. Fatal mistake! They missed an important step in Joshua's plan. They were supposed to wait in the house for "The Package" (Geovana) to arrive, beat her unconscious, make it look like a robbery, break the glass door in the kitchen to show a sign of forced entry, and then leave with a very expensive diamond necklace that Geovana kept in the bedroom.

A hidden obsession with Geovana coupled with an incurable hatred for Joshua compelled Frankie to alter the plan. Although Joshua appeared to be smooth and debonair on the surface, he was really a cold-hearted S.O.B., who didn't give a damn about anyone, particularly when money was involved. Frankie had, on many occasions, experienced Joshua's ruthless problem-solving tactics – both as the witness and the victim. Humiliated, slapped, spit on, and kicked, *Frankie wait patiently for an opportunity to take revenge.*

On the trip back to the airport, Frankie kept repeating, "Revenge is the sweetest joy." They returned the rental car and waited for the hotel shuttle. When they reached the hotel check-in counter, Frankie realized he didn't have his wallet and said, "It must have fallen out of my pocket when you tackled me, you jackass!" They ran outside and jumped in a cab. Alonzo told the cab driver, "23200 West Paloma Blanca Drive, Malibu. Please hurry."

It took almost ninety minutes to make it through the rush hour traffic. Alonzo said, "If she's still unconscious when we arrive, then everything will work out." Geovana awakened as their cab reached the base of the canyon. Her wicked headache made it difficult to dial 9-1-1. When Frankie heard the sirens, he turned around and headed back to the cab, parked just up the street. The ambulance pulled into Geovana's driveway, trailed by several squad cars.

The paramedics treated Geovana and rushed her to the emergency room. An officer noticed Frankie getting into the cab and began walking in their direction. Alonzo said, "Drive!" and immediately contacted the big boss to inform him about the situation. The big boss said, "We'll take care of it," and hung up the phone.

Detective Alvin Johnson of the Los Angeles Sheriff's Department (LASD) arrived at the crime scene. He walked into the house and Officer Smith handed him the assailant's wallet. They also found traces of semen on the bedspread and carpet.

Detective Johnson pulled the driver's license from the wallet, radioed his team and said, "Look for a vehicle with Nevada plates. The assailant is a white male, six foot four inches tall, and two hundred twenty pounds, with black hair, green eyes, and a beard like Abe Lincoln. I am certain that he will return for the wallet."

The officer who saw Frankie get into the cab went inside to tell Detective Johnson. Detective Johnson radioed his team a second time and said, "The car is a green taxi cab – Bell Cab number fifteen seventy-eight."

Further investigation revealed that the assailants had not forced their way into the home. When Detective Johnson checked the doors and windows, they were all locked. Every door, except for the door in the kitchen, had a double cylinder deadbolt and therefore required a key to lock it from the inside. The door in the kitchen had a single cylinder which could be locked or unlocked using your thumb and index finger. Geovana opened this door to let the paramedics into the home.

Detective Johnson began searching for a hidden exit or hallway. After an hour of searching, he re-entered the room where Geovana had been attacked. He discovered a trap door in the floor of the walk-in closet, which led to an underground basement.   The closet had two switches.   One controlled the light on the ceiling.   When he flipped the second switch, at first nothing happened.   Then another officer, collecting a blood sample from the carpet, closed the closet door and a trap door opened.   In the basement, they found a full-scale video production facility.

One of the officers called out, "Hey Detective Johnson.   Take a look at this." He handed the detective a DVD case with a note attached.   The note read, "Make sure you watch this one."   The scene almost made Detective Johnson lose his dinner.   The female star of the adult film was clearly underage. More than five thousand copies of the DVD, various obscene posters of Mrs. Cortez, and computer equipment were confiscated from the premises.

Officers opened the basement exit door, only to find an underground tunnel. The tunnel led to another house on the adjacent street; a house also registered to Joshua Cortez.   Detective Johnson speculated that the assailants had used the tunnel to enter and escape the residence.   However, the assault and rape of Mrs. Cortez puzzled him.

Meanwhile at the hospital, Geovana was slowly recovering.   She had a mild concussion and some swelling.   Dr. Wilson's nurse attempted to contact Mr. Cortez several times with no success.   Geovana finally told the nurse to contact Shari in Atlanta.   The nurse informed Dr. Wilson that Shari would be on the next flight to Los Angeles.

Within a few hours, LASD arrested and took into custody Alonzo James and Frankie Burns for the assault and rape of Geovana Cortez.   Detective Johnson contacted the police officer on duty at the hospital to give Geovana the news.   Detective Johnson also told the officer that he would be coming by the hospital the following morning to ask Mrs. Cortez a few questions.

When Geovana awakened the next day, Shari was there by her bedside, along with Jackson. She was happy to see Shari and surprised to see Jackson. Dr. Wilson informed her that the two men had been taken into custody, and she began crying uncontrollably. Jackson took her hand and whispered, "I'm here for you." But deep inside, he felt helpless. He kept thinking, "Once again I have shown up too late."

Geovana intuitively knew what Jackson was feeling and comforted him by saying, "Baby, it's OK. I'm just happy that you're here. It's not your fault, sweetheart. This time I promise not to let you go!" A single teardrop from his left eye let her know how much he appreciated those words.

Geovana closed her eyes and drifted into a deep sleep. Shari and Jackson went downstairs to get some breakfast. They discussed helping Geovana get back on her feet. "I'm not leaving California without her," Jackson declared. Shari smiled and responded, "I kind of figured you'd say that." They finished eating and headed back to Geovana's room. When they arrived, Detective Johnson was standing outside with two police officers.

Chapter 17

Criminal-minded Acts

News Travels Fast..........................

The Dallas Morning News

National News   September 23, 1999   50 Cents

Teen Pornography Production Studio Discovered In Malibu Residence

08:06 AM CDT on Thursday, September 23, 1999

By LANCE THOMPSON / The Dallas Morning News

During a robbery turned rape investigation on Wednesday, police discovered pornographic materials in an office at the Malibu home of Joshua and Geovana Cortez. Police found more than 4,000 DVDs titled "Rockin' The Cradle: Volume 6." This film features underage teens according to the DVD label and insert.

Authorities are searching for Mr. Cortez. Foul play is suspected and Mr. Cortez is the primary suspect. Two men have been arrested in connection with this case and are being questioned at this time. Mrs. Cortez, who was beaten and raped, is currently hospitalized.

Los Angeles Sheriff's Department (LASD) is offering a $10,000 reward to anyone with information that leads to the capture and arrest of Mr. Joshua Cortez. If you have any information, please contact Detective Alvin Johnson at 1-800-698-8255.

Chapter 18

Geovana Meets Miranda

Possession, Distribution, and Receipt

Are you Mrs. Geovana Cortez?

Yes I am.

Mrs. Cortez, my name is Detective Johnson, and you have the right to remain silent. Anything you say can be used against you in a court of law. You have the right to have an attorney present now and during any future questioning. If you cannot afford an attorney, one will be appointed for you free of charge if you wish.

What do you mean? Are you saying that I'm under arrest? What's going on here? I'm the victim. Why am I under arrest? What did I do wrong?

What's going on here, Officer?

Who are you?

My name is Jackson Gray.

And what is your relationship to Mrs. Cortez?

I am a close friend.

Mrs. Cortez will be taken into custody as soon as the doctor releases her from the hospital.

What did she do? Geovana, who is your attorney?

Benjamin Waters III. You can find his number in the yellow pages under Waters, Steele, and Paxton.

OK. I'll go and contact him right away.

Officers Stone and Bentley: Make sure no one enters or leaves this room without my permission, including her friends. Mrs. Cortez is to have no visitors, I repeat no visitors. As soon as the doctor releases her from this hospital, take her to the station and book her on the following charges:

- 18 USC § 2251. Production of Child Pornography
- 18 USC § 2252. Possession, Distribution and Receipt of Child Pornography

Yes sir, Detective Johnson. We will make sure that no one enters or leaves this room without contacting you first. I will contact you as soon as the doctor releases Mrs. Cortez from the hospital.

No mistakes, Officers. I will be at the precinct going over the evidence. Call me every hour on the hour to give me an update.

Chapter 19

Hotel ZaZa

The Hairline Crack

Detective Johnson arrived at the precinct around 9:45am on Thursday morning. A copy of the Dallas Morning News article about the pornography scandal was on his desk, along with a message to contact Mr. Ron Jenkins immediately at the Hotel ZaZa in Dallas.

214-468-8399

Thank you for calling Hotel ZaZa. This is Sheila. How can I help you?

> Hi, Sheila. My name is Detective Alvin Johnson. I received an urgent message to contact Mr. Ron Jenkins. Is he available?

Yes, he is. Would you mind holding while I page him?

> No, not at all.

Detective Johnson, this is Ron Jenkins. Thank you for returning my call.

> What can I do for you Mr. Jenkins?

I've been informed by Detective Ryan Miller of the Dallas Police Department to contact you regarding the case that you're working in Malibu. Your suspect is here in Dallas at the Hotel ZaZa and your presence is requested here immediately. Arrangements have already been made for you to fly out of LAX today at 12:48pm (US Airways Flight 6942). A return flight will be scheduled for you once you've determined how long you'll be staying for the investigation. When you arrive at the airport, a driver will be waiting to bring you to the hotel. Ask for me at the front desk and I will introduce you to Detective Miller. Do you have any questions?

> Yes I do. What has happened to the suspect?

I've been instructed not to say anything about this case over the telephone. Detective Miller will bring you up to speed once you arrive at the hotel.

I understand, Mr. Jenkins. Thank you for the call and I will see you this evening.

Detective Johnson sat back in his chair with a puzzled look on his face. "What happened in Dallas?" he asked himself. Then the phone rang and he nearly flipped out of his seat. Another officer walking into the room chuckled and said, "You almost busted your ass!" Detective Johnson responded, "Almost!" Then he answered his phone, "Johnson."

Detective Johnson, this is Officer Stone. Mrs. Cortez will be released from the hospital today at 5:00pm.

Great! When you arrive, go ahead and book her. Then take her to the interrogation room for questioning. We'll need to get this done as soon as possible. Has her attorney shown up at the hospital yet?

No, but he has been contacted, according to Mr. Gray, and is on his way.

OK. I will be flying out to Dallas this afternoon. When her attorney arrives, have him contact me immediately. Waters is shrewd and he'll be looking for a way to get the case thrown out on a technicality. Do not answer any of his questions.

No problem, Detective Johnson. What's going on in Dallas?

Not sure. It's something to do with Mr. Cortez. But don't concern yourself with Dallas. Just make sure you don't *ef this up* because Waters will find your mistakes. All he needs is a hairline crack and we can kiss this case goodbye.

Detective Johnson stopped by the evidence room to sign out five of the nude posters linking Geovana to the pornography scandal and headed to the airport.

Chapter 20

Fatal Attraction

Be Careful Who You Pick Up At The Bar!

Detective Johnson arrived at the Dallas Fort Worth airport at 5:40pm on Thursday evening. As promised, a driver from Hotel ZaZa was waiting for him near the baggage claim area. The driver, Antwon Smith, took his bag and the two of them proceeded to the vehicle.

Antwon informed Detective Johnson that Hotel ZaZa was approximately twenty miles away and would take about forty minutes to reach in rush hour traffic. Antwon also asked if he'd ever been to Dallas, and he replied, "No, this is my first time."

During the ride to the hotel, Detective Johnson took some time to review the evidence. He had a hunch that Mrs. Cortez was innocent, although the posters suggested she was involved.

Officers confiscated fifteen different posters of Mrs. Cortez. Some were fully nude and others displayed her modeling lingerie. Most of the posters were a close-up of her vagina, breasts, and buttocks. Each of the posters presenting her from the rear displayed an eye-popping tattoo on the small of her back. "This tattoo looks familiar," Detective Johnson thought.

A team of specialists reviewed seven of the confiscated adult videos and found that Mrs. Cortez did not appear in any of the films. However, Mr. Cortez starred in all except three. Detective Johnson hoped to get some information from Mr. Cortez to confirm his hunch about Geovana. However, he sensed this trip was not about conducting an interrogation; it was about something much more serious.

When Detective Johnson arrived, Mr. Jenkins met him at the front desk. As he suspected, Mr. Cortez was not in a position to be interrogated. The CSI team was onsite collecting evidence and found an unusual note from the person they suspected to be the executioner. Detective Johnson spoke with Detective Miller to get the details of the crime scene.

I entered the hotel room and Detective Miller introduced me as Detective Johnson with the Los Angeles Sheriff's Department. One of the female members of the CSI team removed a note from the evidence bag and informed me that the perfume on the note was Dolce & Gabbana's "Feminine."

It was assumed the executioner wanted us to know a woman had committed this crime. But why? What was her motive? Was she in some way connected to the pornography scandal? I stared at the note which read:

COMPAQ ARMADA 1750 LAPTOP

After a few minutes had passed, I remembered the computer equipment confiscated from the crime scene in Malibu. The laptop bag was present, but the laptop was not. I turned to Mr. Jenkins and asked, "Do you mind if I speak with the members of your staff?" "No, not at all. I'll do whatever it takes to help you resolve this matter."

To his surprise, everyone he needed to speak to was working that night – particularly the front desk clerk and bartender. Detective Johnson went to the front desk first to find out what time Mr. Cortez checked into the hotel.

Hello, Anna Marie. I'm Detective Johnson.   How are you doing tonight?

I'm doing just wonderful, Detective. What can I do to assist you?

I need to know what time Mr. Joshua Cortez checked into the hotel.

No problem. Give me just a moment and I'll look it up on our computer.

While she was looking for the information, Detective Johnson received a call from the police station in Los Angeles. Detective Stone was calling with an update about Mrs. Cortez.

Detective Johnson speaking.

You're not gonna believe what just happened in the interrogation room.

Benjamin Waters III. What did he do?

It's not him this time.

Well, tell me what happened.

You remember the posters we confiscated from the crime scene?

I do . . . And?

Well, Waters demanded that we either provide the evidence being used to detain his client or let her go. So we mentioned the posters and Mrs. Cortez said, "What posters are you talking about?" I responded, "The nude posters." She turned to Waters and said, "I don't know what's going on, but somebody better start explaining why I'm here! Let me see the damn posters - right now!"

And what did you say to her?

I said OK. Waters was present, remember?

Dammit, Officer Stone. Why didn't you call me first?

I did call you...three times. Last time I checked, there weren't any cell phone towers up in the clouds.

OK, wise ass. Then what happened?

We signed out the posters you left behind and brought them into the interrogation room. We asked Officer Sharon Greene to be present for obvious reasons. When Mrs. Cortez saw the posters, she yelled "That's my face but that is not . . . my body! What the hell is going on here, Officers?" Before I could answer, Mrs. Cortez began taking off her clothes. She got up on the table buck naked in a doggie style pose - just as the poster presented - and introduced herself to everyone in the room. She said, "Do you see any resemblance between me and that bitch on the poster? I don't think so." I was feeling a stiff one coming on as I stared in disbelief. For a minute, I thought I was backstage at the Hustler's Magazine convention. In fifteen years on the force, I've never seen anything quite like this.

You've got to be kidding me!

Ha Ha Ha! Had you going there for a minute.

You jackass! What actually happened?

Officer Sharon Greene and Detective Marsha Fields accompanied Mrs. Cortez into a private room to confirm what the posters had revealed. None of the, how can I put this "body parts" matched from the neck down. The woman on the poster had a clit ring and a tattoo on her lower back of two chicks in a sixty-nine position with the words "Do U Like What U C?" Her breasts were much larger and her hips curvier. Since Mrs. Cortez was clearly not the woman on the posters, we let her go, pending further investigation.

I kind of suspected she was innocent! OK. I want a full report on my desk before I return to L.A.

No problem, boss.

Just then, Anna Marie looked up, waved to and called Detective Johnson back to the front desk.

Detective Johnson, I have the information you requested.

OK, Anna Marie. What did you find?

Mr. Joshua Cortez checked in on Tuesday, September 21st at 2:06pm.

Did he have a guest or was he alone?

He was alone. However, I did notice him talking to a woman at the bar.

Please tell me more about this woman.

I would love to, but I only caught a glimpse of her. Her back was turned to me. So I only saw Mr. Cortez. You definitely should talk to Sanchez at the bar. He can probably tell you more about her.

Thanks, Anna Marie, for your time and assistance. You've helped me tremendously.

You know, come to think about it . . . Someone does come here to meet Mr. Cortez, usually on Thursday evening. She's an African-American woman in her late twenties, early thirties, with caramel brown complexion. She's been here several times with Mr. Cortez and usually stays with him through the weekend. Let's see . . . Her name is Cassandra James.

If I produced a photograph, would you be able to identify her?

Definitely! She's about as close to perfect as any woman I've ever seen. You should see how the men lose their freaking minds whenever she goes out to the pool for a swim. And the tattoo on her back . . .

What is it?

It's a picture of two women making out in the sixty-nine position. Underneath the tattoo are the words "Do U Like What U C?" The first time I saw it, I said to myself, "No, she didn't?"

Wow! That's interesting. What time does your shift end?

I leave at eleven. Is there something wrong?

No. You may have just helped me solve an important part of this case. I should have a picture for you to look at before you leave. Thanks again for your cooperation and assistance.

Detective Johnson strolled over to the bar as Sanchez was heading toward the front door. Sanchez had just received an emergency call from his wife that she was on her way to the hospital to deliver their first child. He told Detective Johnson that he'd return to work tomorrow at 4:00pm. Although he didn't like the news, Detective Johnson respected the idea that family comes first.

He returned to the bar and sat for a while, thinking about the tattoo. Alexis Cochran, an intimate friend and business acquaintance had a similar tattoo. The following morning, Detective Johnson received the photo of Cassandra James. That afternoon, Detective Johnson spoke with Sanchez, who described the woman at the bar as Caucasian rather than African-American. Detective Johnson pondered, "I need to get in touch with Alexis."

Chapter 21

The Art of the Deal

Playing Both Sides of the Law

Los Angeles Sheriff's Department Statement Form

DATE: 09/23/1999   TIME: 1:32 a   BADGE #: 76421

NAME: Alonzo James   SUSPECT: ☒ Yes ☐ No
ADDRESS: 9350 Double R Blvd   PH#: 775-331-7854
CITY: Reno, NV 89521   D L #: 0694234
DOB: 07/16/59   POB: Oakland, CA

Above section was entered into the system by the Officer taking the statement.

ADMONITION OF RIGHTS (SUSPECTS ONLY)

You have the right to remain silent. Anything you say can and will be used against you in a court of law. You have the right to talk to an attorney and have an attorney present with you before and during questioning. If you cannot afford an attorney, one will be appointed free of charge to represent you before and during questioning if you desire.

Do you understand each of these rights I have explained to you? ☒ Yes ☐ No

Having these rights in mind, do you wish to talk to us now? ☒ Yes ☐ No

On 09/21/99, I received a phone call from Joshua Cortez to pick up a package at his Malibu office located at 23200 West Paloma Blanca Drive. In the package was a laptop containing important information about the clients and key distributors of WPBD Video Production Company. This laptop is currently in a safe place.

I have read the above statement and find it to be a true and correct summary of the events that occurred.

Bradley Stone
Officer Taking Statement

Alonzo James
Person Giving Statement

Kathryn Lewis
Witness (Print Name)

Kathryn Lewis
Witness (Signature)

Joshua didn't know Alonzo James and Cassandra James were also employed by The Wardlow Clan – an organized crime family out of St. Louis. The Wardlow Clan operated businesses in six states, earning most of their fortune in financial investments and manufacturing. They hired Joshua to manufacture and distribute products to their west coast clients.

Alonzo was trained as Joshua's right hand man and Cassandra his mistress. She quickly peeled away, layer by layer, Joshua's brute and heartless outer shell. Mesmerized by her female prowess and charm, Joshua imprudently gave her access to his financial records, bank accounts, and future plans – plans to cripple and then eliminate the Wardlow Clan.

After receiving this information from Cassandra, the Wardlow Clan ordered the hit on Joshua. Because of the screw-up in Malibu, Alonzo knew he was next if he didn't find a way to get out of jail. So he provided Detective Johnson a partial report from the laptop's database. The full report listed the two-year purchasing history for several city officials, including his police chief. Alonzo said, "I'll give you the laptop and the full report so that you can take down the whole clan. All that I ask is that let me go." Detective Johnson questioned the report's authenticity, but decided to work on a deal.

Chapter 22

A Moral Dilemma

Setting Up The Exchange

What do I do? Chief Brownstone . . . damn! Of all the people to get caught up in something like this. I've known him since I was five, and now I have to . . .

I can't do it. I won't do it. I'll just keep this quiet. Nobody has to know. But I'll know. Can I live with myself if I keep this a secret? But I have to . . . Chief has done so much for me. He's entitled to make a mistake. That's all this is. It's just a misunderstanding. He didn't know what he was purchasing. He didn't know what kind of people he was connected to. I'm sure he intended to do what was right and legal. There's got to be something I can do.

That's it! Dolce & Gabbana's "Feminine." I knew I smelled that fragrance before. Alexis wore it every time we were together. But a contract killer? Hmmm! What if I set up an exchange with Alexis? She wants the laptop and I want these two dirt bags gone for good.

Detective Johnson spent the next three hours trying to track down Alexis. He received a return call from her at 4:35pm. They set up the exchange. At 5:00pm, Alonzo James, accompanied by two police officers, left the precinct and picked up the laptop. While returning, the police cruiser was surrounded at a traffic light by four black Escalades. Alonzo James and the two officers were forced into different vehicles on the left. A man riding in the fourth Escalade retrieved the laptop from the police cruiser's trunk, got back into the vehicle and drove off in a different direction from the motorcade. The officers were handcuffed and blindfolded, but not harmed.

Detective Johnson received a call from Alexis instructing him to bring Frankie Burns to Bakersfield Municipal Airport. She told him, "Come alone and tell no one where you're going. Also bring the partial report and do not make a single copy." When Detective Johnson arrived with Burns, the two police officers were dropped off at an empty parking garage, not too far from the precinct. Before exiting the vehicle, they were shown pictures of their loved ones and told, "Speak about this incident to anyone and your family members die. Understood?" They nodded in agreement.

Meanwhile, somewhere above the Mojave Desert, Alonzo James and Frankie Burns were taking their first skydiving lesson, with no parachute. Alexis forced them to jump from the plane before spraying them with bullets.

Chapter 23

Five Weeks and Counting

How Will Jackson Respond To The News?

404-892-7425

Shari . . . I'm five weeks pregnant.

> That's wonderful news.

No. No. No! It's not wonderful.

> Okay. What's the problem?

It's not Jackson's and it's definitely not Joshua's.

> Oh no! Geo.

Unfortunately, yes. I don't know what to do. You know I don't support abortion, but . . . I honestly don't feel that I will be able to adequately love this child.

> Have you told Jackson?

Are you kidding me? My heart can't take losing him again. He means the world to me and this would crush his spirit.

> Tell him, Geo. The two of you need to make this decision together.

> Yes, it will hurt like hell, but he needs to know.

But what if he decides to leave? He's experienced so much pain because of me. I need him.

> Jackson loves you and I think he'll be OK. Call him right now.

OK. Thanks, Shari. I'll call you later, girl.

Geovana hesitated at first, trying to find a creative way to tell Jackson. Abortion was not an option. Adoption, she considered for about three minutes. Then she speculated what could happen is she raised the child, allowing Jackson to assume Joshua was the father. The weight of guilt made her knees buckle and she fell back onto the sofa, her palms covering her face. There was no way around it. Geovana took Shari's advice and called Jackson.

404-532-7950
Jackson, we need to talk, sweetheart. Call me as soon as possible. Love you, baby.

At first, Jackson was heated, but he never directed his anger toward Geovana. The two of them sat quietly on the couch holding each other for hours. As he held her, he thought, "First jail, then the rape and now this pregnancy. That's supposed to be my baby." Jackson broke his silence, turned to Geovana and said, "I've never felt pain like this before, but I'm with you no matter what. You have my full support." She smiled and said, "Thank you for understanding and loving me," then proceeded to have a conversation with herself.

Geovana, it's OK to feel what you're feeling.

But I've never considered what I'd do in a situation like this. I feel so bad about everything I've done to him.

You know he loves you, right?

I do. But what have I done to deserve his love? When he needed me most, I abandoned him.

He knows your heart. He experienced the best part of you before any of the bad things happened, and he's committed to restoring the relationship. The question is, are you ready to be restored? Are you ready to let go of the past? Remember what Dr. Yuma taught you. Jackson needs you just as much as you need him. He needs your strength. He needs your love.

> Okay, but I still don't understand why Jackson feels this way about me. And how will he be able to love this child, considering the circumstances which brought about my pregnancy?

Geovana decided to keep the baby, and Jackson assured her that he would father the child as his own. Completing Dr. Yuma's counseling sessions as a couple helped them intelligently process the internal war – guilt, self-condemnation, and fear.

Chapter 24

Never Been Loved Like This

Passion . . . Intimacy . . . Restoration

Cleared of all charges in connection with the pornography ring, Geovana relocated to Lake Elsinore - *a quiet and serene community located in Riverside County, roughly seventy-four miles southeast of Los Angeles.* This rental property provided an escape from the reporters and cameras.

Detective Johnson's investigation concluded that each of the actors and actresses, working for Joshua's adult film company, met the minimum age requirement of 18.   The whole operation was nothing more than a masterfully orchestrated marketing campaign.   The database report was authentic, but Detective Johnson swept it under the rug.   With no case to bring to trial, he completed his reports, closed the pornography case and took some time off.

Detective Johnson remained silent about the things he'd learned regarding Alexis, particularly her many disguises and connection to the Wardlow Clan. He knew discussing this information with anyone would certainly result in his death.   Since Geovana posed no threat to their business, the Wardlow Clan left her alone.   However, they did send their real estate agent to purchase both Malibu properties from Geovana.   The Wardlow Clan planned to be fully operational within thirty days and hired two new men to head up the business.   A host of financially strapped political officials were also put on the payroll to prevent the scenario with Joshua from happening again.

Geovana was offered four hundred thousand in cash, a brand new mortgage-free home at the Hamilton Mill subdivision in Dacula, GA, a debt-free slate, and all expenses paid while she settled her business affairs in California.   The two Malibu properties were worth much more, but she couldn't pass on such an attractive opportunity.   Joshua's insurance policy, bank accounts, and real estate provided Geovana an additional six hundred and twenty-five thousand after taxes.

Jackson's home sold in two weeks. He used the profit to cover expenses while he worked full-time on completing his book and training system.

After the closing for the two Malibu properties, Jackson headed to the library and Geovana went grocery shopping. When he arrived at the library, the computers were being used by patrons. He went to the front desk and asked the librarian to look up The Mis-Education of the Negro by Carter G. Woodson. This research ultimately led to Jackson writing the speech which he presented at his Toastmasters club. Psoloman Blacksmith was present for that speech.

Jackson spent the majority of his day reading The Mis-Education of the Negro and taking notes in his journal. He compared his notes from this book to the thirty-two key points that he'd written about the infamous *Willie Lynch Letter*.

He concluded from his research that the basis for most action, by all men, was economic in nature. Shrewd, yet merciless businessmen, sought to dominate and control, by any means necessary, the profit generating activities and enterprises in specific territories or regions – similar to the mindset of gangsters, drug dealers, and certain military-based organizations. Jackson speculated that protecting their economic position meant controlling how and what people learned – a process well documented in the infamous Willie Lynch Letter. He discovered that today's methods for manufacturing the slave mentality had changed, but the motivating factor – *a craving for economic control and domination* – was the same.

Finally, Jackson took notes from the <u>Art of War</u> by Sun Tzu and then turned to a blank page in his journal and wrote in large capital letters, WORTHY OF RESPECT AND ADMIRATION. He suspected that all human beings, not just blacks, had been negatively impacted by manipulative and economically motivated teaching methods – methods still being practiced today.

Jackson wanted to find a way to raise the consciousness of men in the area of economics and spent the next two hours searching for an answer. He hypothesized that current administrators of education would resist any mind development strategy which uncovered the flaws in existing policies and processes. <u>The Art of War</u> helped him understand the importance of pursuing a solution which could be quietly and strategically orchestrated, somewhat like a surprise attack. This approach would ensure and facilitate a smooth transition of economic power from the cutthroats and gangsters to genuine leaders, teachers, and business owners.

At 7:00pm, Jackson returned all the books to the shelves, packed up his study materials, and called his sweetheart.

323-256-9541

Hi, baby, I've been thinking about you all day. How did your research go?

> It went well. I think I have the title for my January Toastmasters speech. We can talk about it later if you're up to it. For now, all that's on my mind is food. I am so hungry. Do you want to go out and grab a bite to eat?

Actually, I've already prepared your favorite meal – Fried Chicken Wings and Collard Greens, Homemade Macaroni and Cheese and Green Beans with Peach Cobbler and Vanilla Ice Cream for dessert.

> For real?

Yes, baby. I'm doing my best to show you how much I appreciate you. I love you! I love you! I love you, Jackson!

> Thank you, sweetheart! You mean the world to me too. I can't wait to get home. Did you get some rest today?

Not really. I want tonight to be special – *something, which will take us well beyond what might be considered romantic* – so I spent the day thinking of you and filling our home with small expressions of love. Will you go on a journey with me?

> Sure! Where are we going?

PARADISE!

> Sounds good to me! Do you need me to stop and pick up anything?

A bottle of wine would be nice...

> What do you have in mind?

Sutter Home Zinfandel California.

> You got it, baby. See you shortly.

OK. Be careful. I love you.

Jackson paused for a moment to think about traveling to *PARADISE* with Geovana. From previous conversations, he knew this meant she was ready to explore intimacy and nurture their sexual relationship. She'd healed well physically. Jackson's care, consideration, and patience helped her stabilize emotionally. They'd also begun attending church service at the Crenshaw Christian Center – home of Dr. Frederick K.C. Price – for spiritual development and enlightenment.

Jackson picked up the two bottles of wine and headed back to Lake Elsinore. When he arrived a little over an hour later, he found Geovana fast asleep. He was disappointed; in fact, he was pissed off.

I sat down at the table and began consuming the first bottle of wine with my dinner. The thought of being intimate with Geovana was so overwhelmingly fascinating, that it caused me to act selfishly. Then I remembered what Mr. Richardson told me, "Find Geovana, repair her broken heart and give her the love that she's never known." Before long, I found myself making a small bed on the floor in front of the couch where Geovana slept. Before I drifted off to sleep, I carefully studied every detail of her lovely face. What a beautiful sight.

Around 1:00am, I woke up with Geovana lying down beside me. The journey to *PARADISE* began with a gentle kiss. She then apologized for falling asleep. I responded, "Shhh! It's okay, baby. I understand. Dinner was wonderful. The only thing missing was you. Let's try again tomorrow evening."

She thanked me for being a gentleman and assured me that our love would never be interrupted again. I smiled and said, "Are you in the mood to talk?" She responded, "Sure! Why not?" Then I asked her to tell me more about the journey to *PARADISE.* Her response, "I can show you better than I can tell you."

My shirt was the first thing to go. Geovana reached for the bottle of massage oil on the end table and began erasing the tension from my shoulders and back. Then I returned the favor after affectionately helping her get undressed - everything except her panties. There's something about saving the best part for last, which has always excited me. And since I enjoy taking my time with intimate matters, Geovana was thrilled and ready to explore a night of pleasure.

I could feel her tremble with each knead and caress of her soft caramel brown skin. When I began massaging her feet, she let out a long sigh and a tear of appreciation for my consideration and patience. She told me, "I know it's been difficult for you to wait. It means a lot to me. Thank you."

Before another tear could fall, I kissed her gently from the bottom of her cheek up to her left eye. The way she looked into my eyes penetrated me deeply. Without speaking a word, Geovana had introduced me to the meaning of *PARADISE* - a place of extreme beauty, delight, and happiness.

Then she surprised me with the ultimate gift. She spoke in a seductive tone, "How long do you want to remain the man of my dreams and love of my life?" I answered, "Forever, baby!" Without hesitation, she reached under the sofa and pulled out a small box. Inside was a hand written note and a picture of an engagement ring. The note read, "Will you marry me, Jackson Dwayne Gray?" We sat there looking into each other's eyes for what seemed like hours. The smile on our faces indicated we were in agreement to spend our lives together. Then she recited from memory a poem she'd written for me shortly after moving to California.

> There's no comparison
> Blinded by my own pain
> I struggle daily to regain
> My courage and my strength
> Believing that one day
> The touch of your hands
> Will awaken me
> To your face and your smile

We spent the next few days shopping for the perfect ring. The remainder of the early morning hours was filled with passion, intimacy, and restoration.

We became one.

Chapter 25

A Change of Scenery

Jackson and Geovana Visit Family and Friends

Geovana and Jackson decided to begin their transition to Atlanta during the Christmas holidays. They both wanted to be with family and friends to bring in the millennium. The Y2K bug had been the main topic of discussion for the last few months. While no significant computer failures occurred when the clocks rolled over into the year 2000, preparation for the Y2K bug had a huge impact on businesses around the globe.

After celebrating Christmas and New Year's Day with family and friends, it was back to business for Jackson. His first project for the year was a speech at his Toastmasters Club – Charismatic Communicators. He presented the speech he'd written in California titled "We Are Worthy of Respect and Admiration." This speech set in motion a series of transformative events for Psoloman, which, consequently, positioned him to be invited as the keynote speaker at the 2003 Toastmasters International Conference.

Geovana met with Dr. Yuma before returning to Atlanta, and he offered her a position on his team. Since he was planning to relocate to Atlanta within the next four months, Geovana took on the responsibility of finding the perfect location for his second counseling facility. She found it in an upscale section of Duluth, Georgia, and began meeting with contractors to transform the office space into a replica of the California location.

Initial construction of their new home in Dacula was underway. They returned to California for two weeks in April to finalize personal and business affairs, set up Geovana's remaining clients with other trusted real estate professionals, and meet with Dr. Yuma to bring him up to date on the second counseling facility.

Seven months pregnant, with twins, Geovana's energy level was unusually high. She paid close attention to her diet and walked daily for exercise. Jackson did all he could to make her comfortable and minimize stress. Still, she wondered if Jackson was ready to be their father.

Chapter 26

Teammates For Life

Dr. Yuma's Move To Atlanta, GA

Moving to Atlanta was the best decision I'd made in years. I get to see my children, Emily and Ricardo, everyday - thanks to Geovana. She not only facilitated the entire project of constructing my second counseling facility in Atlanta, but also found me the perfect home. It's within walking distance of Mariella's place, allowing me to enjoy dinner and sleep-overs with my children. They have their own rooms at both homes and are excited about me living in Atlanta. Mariella and I have developed a healthy relationship since the divorce and share the responsibility of providing for and raising our children.

The counseling practice, Teammates For Life, has made a significant impact on the quality of life for couples throughout the Atlanta area, particularly in Gwinnett, Dekalb, and Fulton counties. Unlike the facility in Los Angeles, we added a wellness center to the Duluth location. To support the wellness project, I began working out five times a week and changed my eating habits. Shortly before my transition from Thousand Oaks to Atlanta, my trainer at Gold's Gym gave me a list of exceptional fitness trainers and wellness experts.

I decided to train with Tai Lynn – a fitness champion and business system development consultant. It was something about her attention to detail and genuine concern for her clients that attracted me. Watching her conduct the kickboxing class also worked in her favor.

Tai Lynn uses a modified version of the Body 4 Life routine to help her clients quickly reduce body fat, while building lean muscle and increasing endurance. I dropped forty-five pounds and six pants sizes during our first year working together. Today, I primarily eat fish and poultry, along with an assortment of vegetables. I've completely eliminated pork, beef, junk food and most sweets from my diet. I still crave ice cream and visit the Cold Stone Creamery at least once a week, usually with my children.

Outside of the gym, Tai Lynn attends my small group on *A Course In Miracles (ACIM)* every Tuesday at 7:00pm. She was a little apprehensive at first, but decided to give it a try after reading Marianne Williamson's book <u>A Return To Love</u>. Tai Lynn's spiritual background is *Tao Te Ching* and *The Science of Mind*. She attended the first meeting alone. For the second visit, she brought two guests – her husband Kado and best friend Kaiya.

Kado, a student of *Dr. Wayne Dyer*, sat quietly and studied everyone as they asked and answered various questions. He thought the hugging was a bit excessive, but participated out of respect.

Kaiya really enjoyed the experience. She and Tai Lynn facilitate a women's health and wellness study group, combining *The Science of Mind* with Tai Lynn's fitness program.

I wasn't romantically interested in Kaiya until I observed her preparing for the Ms. Fitness Competition. Her determination was fascinating. I arrived at the gym earlier than usual, and she was training with Tai Lynn. The two of them were completing an intense cardio workout. When she saw me standing at the door, she smiled and signaled for me to come inside.

As I approached Kaiya, she reached for my hand and asked, "What are you doing in about an hour?" I said, "Not sure. What do you have in mind?" She replied, "Hot tea. Would you care to join me?" I said, "Absolutely!" We've been in love ever since. Thirty days later, I asked her to be my wife, and she accepted.

Kaiya Sinclair Yuma

Chapter 27

Still Concerned

Geovana's Insecurities About Jackson

My value on Dr. Yuma's team had been established and proven. I'd grown emotionally and developed an uncompromising self-love. We'd planned our wedding, inviting close to one hundred and seventy-five people.

Jackson and I had thoroughly discussed our responsibility as parents and were happy to have the opportunity. Even spiritually, we'd reached a level of consciousness and unity unknown by most couples. Throughout the pregnancy, we read books together, attended parenting courses, went shopping, and prepared our home. Though thankful for Jackson, I still *didn't know* how he felt about my pregnancy and desperately needed to.

Jackson just wanted healthy children. I wanted him to love these babies as his own - to name our children. Sure, he'd look through books with me and searched the internet, but never suggested any names. I felt like Jackson secretly hated me for making this decision, even though all he showed me was his love. He'd say things like, "I'm not sure. Names are important. I don't want to make a mistake. What names do you like?" In my mind, it all translated into the same thing, "You selfish . . . How I could you go through with this pregnancy, given the circumstances?"

I tried my best to understand and be considerate, since Jackson wasn't the natural father. He continuously reminded me that I had his full support. But for some reason, his words alone weren't enough to satisfy my need to know that he was going to be okay.

On June 1, 2000, my contractions intensified. Jackson was returning from a meeting in downtown Atlanta. Since it was rush hour, Shari took me to the hospital. She had recently married and was expecting her first child. After selling both homes, they purchased a larger house just a few driveways down from us. Having Shari close by was comforting. Plus, our children would grow up together.

Once we were in the car, Shari handed me a box wrapped in baby paper. I said, "Shari, you didn't have to." She said, "I didn't." I removed the wrapping paper. Inside, a handwritten note from Jackson titled 25 Reasons YILOVEU. The package also contained a pink and a blue baby bib. Andrea Rene and Alexander Ramon were embroidered on them. I smiled. It was exactly what I needed.

When we arrived, Jackson was already there. He'd been planning this surprise for several months. I asked him, "What's going on, sweetheart? Why is Dr. Yuma here?" He answered, "I'm doing what's necessary to make our family complete. Will you marry me today? Right here, right now?" I responded, "What about the wedding?" Jackson said, "This moment is for Andrea and Alexander. December is for everyone else." Dr. Yuma performed the ceremony and our twins were born just before midnight.

Chapter 28

The Librarian

Her Knight In Shining Armor

When Psoloman arrived home, Antoinette was there waiting for him. She usually stopped by after class, and they'd share their daily experiences. Many of these conversations lasted for hours. On nights when she couldn't stop by, Antoinette talked with Psoloman on the phone.

She fascinated Psoloman because she listened intently and asked questions about his passion. He fascinated Antoinette because he always treated her as his queen. He opened her door, watched his tone, showed her affection, rubbed her feet, and took his time loving her, making it easy for her to be free in his company.

Since meeting him online, her life has changed completely. Initially, she was a bit apprehensive with meeting someone through a dating service. With so many horror stories from online daters, Antoinette put it off as long as she could. She kept company with two guys during the previous six years, neither wanting to commit. Finally, Antoinette decided to remain single and celibate until she met someone ready to settle down and start a family.

After dating Antoinette for only ten weeks, Psoloman gave her the biggest surprise of her life. It was March 3, 2003. The day had been perfect. It was sunny and bright with an average temperature of seventy-five degrees. No showers or thunderstorms had been forecast. The flowers were beginning to bloom and the air was refreshing.

Antoinette had been a director for Gwinnett Public Library since 2002. Her extensive training and background in the library system, as well as her awesome research and presentation skills, helped her secure the top position. She and her friend Russ spent several weeks creating a video presentation of the library's history. Antoinette became not only the first

African-American, but also the first female, director in the Gwinnett County Public Library System.

Psoloman visited the library at least once a week to take Antoinette out for lunch. Her staff members were always excited to see him. They were especially happy on this wonderful day in March. Psoloman had already spoken to her grandparents about his plans, and they approved. Her grandfather only requested that Psoloman and Antoinette register for and attend the 12-week marriage seminar at his church. Psoloman honored his request and signed up the same day.

The following Monday, Psoloman arrived at the library at 12:05pm. Maggie greeted him a hug. He pulled her aside and showed her the surprise. Filled with excitement, she asked, "How can I help?" Maggie gathered the entire staff and then called Antoinette to the Circulation Desk. Psoloman went out to his car to get the dozen long-stem roses.

When he walked through the door and saw Antoinette's smile, Psoloman knew it was the beginning of a wonderful life. He presented her the roses, and she gave him a big hug. Then, with her entire staff gathered, as well as some of the patrons, he went to one knee. Her smile changed to an "Oh my God!" Psoloman opened the ring box and said, "Antoinette, you are a source of light in my life, my inspiration, my friend, and my love. Will you also be my wife?" Antoinette stared at the ring and then at Psoloman. She went back and forth several times. Psoloman waited patiently for her response. Then he whispered, "Baby, are you okay?" She looked into in his eyes and responded, "Yes, I'm okay and yes, I will marry you!" Everyone started clapping and congratulating the two of them.

Antoinette Hodges

Chapter 29

A Well Orchestrated Plan

Psoloman's Trip To The Bookstore

Although I had nothing pressing scheduled for a few hours, I was hoping to get home by 6:00pm. I counted three automobile accidents within the same half mile. Luckily, no one was seriously injured.

Traffic at a standstill, I remembered that <u>Daredevil</u> featuring Ben Affleck had just been released. Since Antoinette was a huge fan, I got off the freeway at the next exit and headed to the bookstore. As I entered the Barnes and Noble, I was drawn to a large poster with a familiar face. It was my friend from California, Dr. Takoda Yuma. He had a book signing scheduled that evening at 6:30pm. I purchased a copy of <u>Daredevil</u> and Takoda's book, waiting patiently to see my friend and have it signed.

"G"

Seven Characteristics of God Which Nurture

Healthy and Lasting Relationships

A Novel

Dr. Takoda Yuma

and

Geovana Gray

G: *Seven Characteristics of God Which Nurture Healthy and Lasting Relationships* © **2003 Takoda Yuma and Geovana Gray**

Published by **Antwan Goodwin Publishing**
Visit our Website at **www.WeKnowRelationships.com**

This is a work of fiction. Although certain incidents described herein are based on actual events, all of the characters – with the exception of well-known public figures referred to by name – are products of the author's imagination and are not to be construed as real. In all but the obvious respects, any resemblance to actual persons living or dead, business establishments, events or locales is entirely coincidental.

Limit of Liability/Disclaimer of Warranty: While the publisher and author have used their best efforts in preparing this book, they make no representations or warranties with respect to the accuracy or completeness of the contents of this book and specifically disclaim any implied warranties of merchantability or fitness for a particular purpose. No warranty may be created or extended by sales representatives or written sales materials. The advice and strategies contained herein may not be suitable for your situation. You should consult with a professional where appropriate. Neither the publisher nor author shall be liable for any loss of profit or any other commercial damages, including but not limited to special, incidental, consequential, or other damages.

Library of Congress Cataloging-in-Publication Data

G: Seven Characteristics of God Which Nurture Healthy and Lasting Relationships: a

novel / Takoda Yuma and Geovana Gray

      p.   cm.

1. Jacobs, Malachi (Fictitious Character) – Fiction.   2. Cultural Diversity – Fiction. 3.

Intimate Relationships – Fiction   4. Spiritual Awareness - Fiction   5. Sexuality - Fiction

      I. Title.

      ISBN 0-1234-9876-2

      Printed in the United States of America

The G Logo is a registered trademark of Men and Women of INFLUENCE, LLC. For information regarding special discounts for bulk purchases, please contact the MWI Sales Team at 404-409-5144 or Sales@MWITrainingSystem.com

Psoloman was fascinated with the G-Logo. Before starting the first chapter, he looked up each of the seven words in a dictionary and briefly reviewed the underlying principles for the nine spiritual books. He was intrigued by the Bible verse wrapping the outside of the G-Logo, especially the part which read, "And though all its parts are many, they form one body." Psoloman strongly considered using the Bible verse as a basis for the introduction in his book titled <u>Mixed Nuts</u>. He'd been working with an agent for over a year to get a book publishing deal.

After the book signing, Psoloman headed home. He read the first three chapters of the book before Antoinette arrived. He and Antoinette discussed what he'd learned, particularly about one of the characters in the second chapter.

Chapter 1 - Welcome To S.A.R.A.H.

Hello everyone! My name is Rosalyn Simone and I'm the Facility Coordinator at S.A.R.A.H. I will be leading you on a tour of the facility and helping you get settled into your respective rooms. S.A.R.A.H. is a 7-day retreat facility for heterosexual couples. During your stay, you'll learn how to cultivate what we refer to as the Intimacy Factor. That is, how to express words, which edify, encourage, and stimulate life in your partner. The Intimacy Factor allows you to look into each other's eyes and see a beauty that can't be described. It makes the sexual pleasure last well beyond the orgasm.

This week's class includes 20 couples from different cities and states around the U.S. Together, your group represents 7 nationalities, 5 spiritual paths or religions, with ages ranging from 22 to 51.

Approximately 75% of the couples who attend the 7-day retreat go on to create a phenomenal life together. We receive letters all the time from couples sharing how well our training program works. Here's a letter we received last week:

Dear Mr. and Mrs. Jacobs,

We don't know how to thank you for helping us save our marriage. We were convinced your program would do nothing for us. All we did was argue with each other about the stupidest things. At first, it was difficult to embrace relationship-building insight from so many perspectives.

We learned to appreciate the incredible value found in diversity; not only in religion, but also in the dynamics two people bring to the relationship. This shift in our thinking has been the greatest contributor to the success of our marriage, as well as our relationships with friends, family, and co-workers. We believe that the Intimacy Factor is a profound strategy for cultivating healthy and loving relationships. We've recommended S.A.R.A.H. to all of our friends. Thanks a million!

With Great Love and Respect,
William and Stephanie Marshall

Psoloman paused for a moment to ponder the point about diversity. He began to consider how he'd grown over the past three years. Psoloman realized, in that moment, how people from all walks of life had shaped him into the man he'd become.

Chapter 2 - Day One

Good morning, class! Let me formally introduce myself. My name is Malachi Jacobs. I will be your guide and counselor during your stay at S.A.R.A.H. I sincerely hope you are well rested and ready to have a great time.

We noticed most of you reading the "Welcome To S.A.R.A.H." sign after exiting the bus. In addition to the information presented on the sign, we want you to know this is not your typical spiritual retreat. We are here to celebrate life and marriage. We consider marriage to be the ultimate union - a sacred union that has been mishandled and abused by men and women alike. Marriage has been made to appear to be unattractive, usually by individuals with poor relationship-building skills. Fortunately, some of us know that marriage provides phenomenal benefits to couples who know how to cultivate intimacy.

To have intimacy in a relationship, the two people must first learn the difference between two important concepts – musts haves and preferences.

Must Haves are biological human needs. They can't be ignored. Much of the discomfort and disappointment individuals experience in their marriage is due to misunderstanding this concept. Must Haves, when satisfied, offer the highest form of security and position each partner to contribute significant value to the other.

Preferences on the other hand are simply wants, and oftentimes, have a prejudicial root. Preferences place unreasonable demands on the other person. These demands eventually cultivate resistance. Why? Because it ignores the law of reciprocity.

Marriage is a high quality exchange; it's a give and receive, with very specific requirements. Learn these requirements or Must Haves, and you'll be a delight to your spouse. Ignore them and there's hell to pay. Biological needs don't simply go away. The urge to satisfy Must Haves becomes stronger when they're ignored or neglected, compelling the individual to seek new means of satisfaction. Enter infidelity; abuse; aggression; disregard.

My staff and I intend to lead you on a journey into authentic and fulfilling relationship. Our techniques will help you protect your marriage from the ignorance that each of us experiences before we learn how to satisfy Must Haves. Please have an open mind, because you'll be exposed to teachings from the Holy Bible, Holy Koran, Science of Mind, The Supreme Mathematics, *A Course In Miracles (ACIM)*, The Scientology Handbook, Talmud, Bhagavad Gita, and Tao Te Ching. It is not our goal or intent to convert you to a new religion. We will simply expose you to the proven methods and techniques each of these doctrines suggest for cultivating a healthy and loving relationship.

It doesn't matter if you've been together twenty-five years or twenty-five days, your experience at S.A.R.A.H. will completely change your perspective about what it takes to nurture and cultivate the best relationship. You'll develop the skills which grant you greater access to each other's heart and mind. As a result, you'll be able to create and experience a relationship that is pleasant and fulfilling.

Are you excited about this possibility? Great! Let's get started. First things first. Gentlemen, please say goodbye to the ladies. We will not see them again until the formal dinner and dancing event this evening. They will be training with my wife, Rebekah Jacobs.

While we discuss sexuality, romance and lovemaking, they will receive facials, massages, manicures, and pedicures. Tonight they will look their absolute best, and each of you will show up as the gentleman they long for in their lives. Any questions?

Now that the ladies have gone, let's have a serious talk. First, I want to break the ice with unbiased conversation about what it means to be a man. Thoughtfully consider the words in the following poem about how nature transforms us into men:

The Making of a Man

When Nature wants to make a man, her methods are unconventional. Her goal is to perfect him and make him a worthwhile leader - first leading himself, then his family, and finally others.

She breaks him into pieces through the circumstances of life, and then puts him back together again, accurate and precise. Not any man will do; a certain manner of man is required, a man who can stand the fire, a man with a Godly desire. He's someone with a great purpose, whose vision sees beyond his eyes; she inspires him through wisdom, intelligently removing all the lies. She'll do what she must do to make this man brand new, like Genesis 1:26, a reflection of the truth. His genius she ignites, his power she magnifies, giving him wisdom and life, in exchange for ignorance and pride. She keeps him wanting more by satisfying his unfulfilled needs; with confidence and great intent, he pursues his highest dreams.

Do I have any men in the room today who reflect the quality of man illustrated by this poem? This is not an attack. This is not an attempt to make you look foolish or incompetent. I ask this question because this is the type of man our wives ache for, long to touch and care for.

There's a spiritual calling in a woman for a man who operates in this capacity. The first thing we must do as men is exercise our faith, and faith demands that we ask God for instruction, wisdom, and direction.

It's comical that men typically will not ask for directions, even when we're lost. A woman knows that to ask for direction means to stop being lost, to stop driving in circles, and to begin making progress.

The Bible teaches us in the Book of James chapter 1 verse 5, "If any of you lacks wisdom, he should ask God, who gives generously to all without finding fault . . ."

The Book of Proverbs states in chapter 3 verses 5 and 6, "5Trust in the LORD with all your heart and lean not on your own understanding; 6in all your ways acknowledge Him and He will make your paths straight."

Gentlemen, we desire that our women submit to us, and it is completely natural for them to do so. However, her submission is not to you, but to the characteristics of God which you embody and express in a loving way. Until we learn to submit to and become like God, we cannot reasonably expect our wives to align with us. Their submission is to God; it is how they were designed. And though God created her to be a man's companion and teammate, He did not give man permission to handle her at his discretion.

God is ready to teach us how to handle a woman with care, skill, love, and respect. He's ready to teach us how to draw out of woman her natural desire to submit and support. However, God's system is orderly and there are prerequisites that must be satisfied before certain changes come about. The first step is for man to develop a relationship with God to initiate his own transformation.

Who is bold and mature enough to ask God for help? Everyone? Great! Let's continue the journey.

Today's Characteristic of God is **BE GENTLE.** Society has not taught men the importance of being gentle, and therefore, we apply pressure, when and where pressure is not required. We will begin the process of undoing the thought system that makes men intolerable.

To be <u>gentle</u> means to deliberately or voluntarily express kindness and self-control when dealing with others; easily managed or handled; not steep or sudden; gradual. The keyword is KINDNESS.

In 1966, singer Otis Redding released a beautiful song titled "Try A Little Tenderness." According to my research, Mr. Redding did not want to record this song. It was the encouragement of executives and friends which persuaded him to reconsider. Still not convinced the record would sell, he sang it in a way to ensure it would not be released. However, the ploy didn't work and "Try A Little Tenderness" became his signature song and top selling record.

Men, I respectfully ask each of you to try a little tenderness. The ladies are being pampered, massaged, caressed and comforted as we speak. In what ways do you pamper, massage, caress and comfort the woman in your life? Does she feel good when she's in your company?

This afternoon, we will visit the spa to experience what it is like to be served, as well as how to serve our wives. Any questions on what we've covered so far? No questions? Superb! Let's take a 15 minute break. When we return, we'll talk about pleasing a woman sexually. Please be back in the room no later than 11:15am.

While sitting in the waiting room at the spa, Rebekah asked the ladies a simple question: "How often do you take time to prepare yourself to look, feel, and smell beautiful for your husband? If you're not doing it, every charming and provocative woman he encounters will steal a small piece of him away from you. Eventually, his mind will become accustomed to and influenced by these encounters, emotionally rendering you less and less attractive to him."

Lisa, one of the younger women in the group, resisted the idea at first, but was quickly persuaded by Ellen's story about her first husband.

Anthony was the perfect husband and friend. However, I was so busy working on my career that I forgot to protect and nurture my relationship. When I got pregnant with Jonathon, Anthony and I decided that he'd stay home and raise our son. I made almost triple his salary, and we enjoyed the lifestyle it had afforded us.

Things were fine for the first two years, so it seemed. I'd leave home before 7:00am and work until seven or eight at night. Anthony tried, on many occasions, to talk to me about feeling lonely, and he wanted us to spend more time together. I always responded that we had bills to pay, and I was the only one working.

Eventually, he stopped talking about what he felt, and I figured he'd finally begun to see things my way. He and Jonathon continued to build their relationship, and I increased my workload in order to double my commissions and secure the top sales position.

Three years later, Anthony and Jonathon were gone when I arrived home. The judge granted Anthony full custody, leaving me alone and heartbroken. On top of that, I'm still paying three thousand dollars each month for alimony and child support.

Anthony had been seeing a counselor for over a year, doing all he could to save our marriage. My behavior appeared to the judge as neglect and worked in Anthony's favor. And then, of course, there was Liz. Liz McKay, the man-stealing, low-down, hypocritical bitch next door!

She was a work-at-home mom running a business from her basement. Her husband spent most days on the road, as regional director for a large corporation. Their love appeared genuine and they expressed their affection publicly. But apparently, she was having the same marital problems as Anthony.

Since I'd known Anthony to be a man of his word, I didn't consider Liz to be a threat. They would take the boys to the park, story time, and other places children enjoyed going. What I couldn't see was the connection Anthony and Liz had begun to cultivate, due to my absence in his life. Anthony never cheated with her sexually, as far as I know. However, he did stop fighting for our relationship, and I believe my actions encouraged him to give up.

Though I'm happily married to Kevin, I miss my son's smile. I miss walking into his room each morning to kiss him goodbye. It's been ten long years since they walked out on me, and it still hurts like hell.

Tears began to form in the eyes of all the women, as they listened to Ellen share her experience. Lisa walked over to Ellen and gave her a hug and some tissue. They all sat quietly for a while.

At 11:15am sharp, the men were seated and ready to discuss how to please a woman sexually. The first man to speak was a twenty-eight year old African-American from Atlanta, Georgia.

Hello! My name is Jackson Gray.

When Psoloman read this, he couldn't believe it. Although he wasn't sure if this was the same Jackson Gray, in a flash, Psoloman was back at Toastmasters. Meeting Jackson had unintentionally provoked Psoloman to pursue his passion for uniting people.

Psoloman put the book down and walked over to the window. With penetrating focus and overwhelming gratitude, he looked into the sky and said, "Thank you, God!" Psoloman closed his eyes and said a prayer before returning to the story. "Heavenly father, only You could orchestrate such a brilliant plan. I'm not sure where we're headed, but I'm glad You chose me. And thank you for sending me such a lovely companion. Amen!"

After his prayer, Psoloman poured a glass of water and returned to the story.

Hello! My name is Jackson Gray. I've been thinking about this topic for some time now. Geovana and I dated initially during high school and reunited in 1999. We remained celibate as teenagers and recently began to explore the idea of sexual intimacy as a couple.

Geovana has been through some traumatic experiences and asked me to take things slow.   As far as an intimate relationship, she's been searching for something greater, something spiritual, something God-inspired. She calls it PARADISE. We're not even sure what it is, but continue to pursue its meaning as a team.

With that said, I believe pleasing a woman sexually requires unbiased support and consideration for her past hurts and fears, as well as her personal growth and triumphs. Today's Characteristic of God says it all – BE GENTLE.

Bob, Jimmy, and Richard also shared their perspectives about how to satisfy a woman sexually. They presented a typical male dominated experience, relying mostly upon endurance, size, and intensity. The instructor concluded the discussion by saying, "All of you are right if that's what the woman in your life enjoys. Talk to her often. Kindly ask her questions and then listen. Let her teach you not only how to please her sexually, but also how to love her in a way that stimulates her to submit to the vision you've established with God for your family."

After the discussion, the men went to lunch and met at the spa at 2:30pm. To their surprise, the spa treatments were just what they needed.

Each of the couples arrived at the formal dinner looking radiant and revitalized. Dinner was exceptional and the dancing . . . wonderful! The couples talked, laughed, and tastefully entertained the thought of a night filled with passion and intense orgasms. Malachi and Rebekah joined the couples on the dance floor. Shortly before the party was over, Malachi announced, "Tomorrow's session begins at 1:00pm sharp. Have fun and discover what it's like to spend the morning with the person you love. Good night!"

Chapter 3 - Day Two

Good afternoon, class! The music last night was nice, during and after the party. Isn't the sexual experience sweeter when you handle each other gently and take your time?

To be gentle is to apply love and God is love according to the Book of First John chapter 4 verse 8. How many of you have ever invited God into your bedroom, into your sexual experience? If you haven't, I challenge you to stop and say a prayer together, inviting God to guide each of you through to ecstasy and fulfillment. Rebekah and I have practiced this for years and, believe me, it makes a difference.

Today's Characteristic of God is **BE GENUINE.** Society has not taught men the importance of being genuine, and therefore, we hide our true feelings behind the so-called strength. Today, we will begin the process of undoing the thought system that makes men insensitive and heartless.

To be gentle means to be free from hypocrisy or dishonesty; not pretended; sincerely felt or expressed. The keyword is FREE.

When you are free, it's much easier to be honest about your thoughts and feelings. Most men neglect their feelings and, as a result, become insensitive to the feelings of others.   To be sensitive is not an indication of weakness, but of power and self-control.

Geovana raised her hand and asked, "How does a woman learn to enjoy intimacy again, after she's been robbed of her innocence by a rapist?"
Rebekah responded, "Not easily. It takes time, prayer, and a patient, loving husband." During the break, Rebekah approached Geovana and suggested

they take a walk. Geovana said, "Sure, why not! Let me tell Jackson."
Rebekah replied, "Malachi has already informed him."

The two of them talked about Rebekah's experience in college, where she
was raped. Rebekah didn't ask Geovana to share what had happened to her.
Instead she allowed Geovana to listen to how she navigated her way back to
love. Geovana cried until there were no more tears. Rebekah consoled and
assured her that she was going to be alright. Geovana smiled.

That evening, Geovana read poetry and made love to Jackson. She told him,
"No one has ever touched me so gently and respectfully. Instead of
removing the clothes from my body, you've removed the veil from my eyes.
You are my true love."

The meaning of PARADISE was becoming clearer each day.

Chapter 30

Breakfast At Mimi's

The Bridge To A Lifelong Friendship

Before leaving the bookstore, Psoloman spoke with Dr. Yuma. He hadn't seen him in five years, but they reconnected as if no time had passed. After an interesting, yet brief, discussion, they settled for a breakfast meeting the following Tuesday at Mimi's Cafe.

During their meeting, Psoloman learned about *A Course In Miracles (ACIM)* and how it had changed Dr. Yuma's life. Psoloman committed to attending Dr. Yuma's study group to learn more about *A Course In Miracles (ACIM)*. He also confirmed that the Jackson Gray he'd met at Toastmasters was the same character in Dr. Yuma's novel.

A few weeks later, Psoloman received a package in the mail from Jackson Gray. Inside was a signed copy of Jackson's new book My Money Works For Me. An audio CD accompanied the book, along with Jackson's business card. Psoloman contacted Jackson immediately.

404-532-7950

Hello, you have reached the voice mailbox for Jackson Gray. Your call is important to me, and I will return your call as soon as time allows. At the sound of the beep, please leave your name, number, and your reason for calling. Thank you and have a phenomenal day. Beeeeeeeeeep!

Hey there, Jackson. It's Psoloman Blacksmith. I received your package and wanted to say thank you. Also, I'd like to meet with you to talk about your book and your January 2000 Toastmasters speech. My number is 678-859-1499. Look forward to hearing from you. Have a great day!

Chapter 31

Leaving A Legacy

Psoloman Begins To Pave The Way For Future Generations

678-859-1499

Hello, this is Psoloman.

Psoloman, it's Jackson Gray. How have you been doing, man?

Great! Many positive things have happened since we first met three years ago.

It's been a similar experience for me.

I'm excited about what you're doing. <u>My Money Works For Me</u> is amazing. I've read six chapters and, though I'm not brilliant with numbers, the content was clearly written and easy to follow. The worksheets and charts were definitely a plus.

Yeah. Building wealth is simple. People just need to be taught the rules of money in a language they can understand and practice.

I know what you mean. By the way, is Geovana Gray your wife?

As a matter of fact, she is. We tied the knot on June 1, 2000.

She's a beautiful lady. I spoke to her at the book signing for <u>G</u>. When I read your name in the story, I was like, Whoa!

It was me. Geovana and Dr. Yuma have been working together for a few years now. They decided to write the novel shortly after Geovana and I returned from S.A.R.A.H. Malachi and Rebekah Jacobs were amazing facilitators and they have an exceptional marriage.

Have you and Geovana found Paradise yet?

We've just begun to scratch the surface, but even at this early stage, the experience is astounding. Paradise is like being filled with the presence of some magnificent power and intelligence. Everything we do together just works when we allow it to guide us. It's almost spooky how quickly things unfold. Initially, we move into a state of unequivocal peace. Then our emotional state transitions into a realm of suspended ecstasy, even when sex is not our objective.

Interesting! How do you gain access to Paradise?

> Exactly the way Malachi explained it in the novel. Stop and say a prayer to initiate the connection. Once we're fully present for each other, the slightest touch is electrifying. Malachi was speaking of a sexual encounter in his example, but Geovana and I have had success inviting this presence into other areas of our lives.

By presence, are you referring to God?

> God, Allah, Jehovah, Jah, Lord, Most High, Elohim, Great Spirit, Infinite Intelligence, Father, The Great I AM. He is the Supreme One who governs the universe and everything in it, including you and me.

Wow! You have grown significantly. What's been the most significant contribution to your growth?

> The Bible, Supreme Mathematics, Science of Mind, and teachings from Crown Financial Ministires.

Since you mentioned the Bible first, is it correct to assume that you're a Christian?

> It depends on how you define Christian. It's my preference to live without titles because titles have a tendency to separate people and open the door to judgment. We both know that he who judges others is judged by others. I truly believe that God flows in and through me like blood and oxygen. He is with me everywhere I go.
>
> If I were to give my spiritual life a title, it would be SONOFGOD. I learned about this perspective through an intense study of the Book of Romans, chapter 8. The Spirit of Life set me free. I strive to make my mind one with the Spirit who dwells within me - the part of me which is a direct reflection of the Supreme One. When I am led by the Spirit of God, I am a son of God, according to the Bible. If

being a Christian reflects what I've just shared, then I am a Christian.

I see.

By the way, I will be sharing the stage with you next week, at the 2003 Annual Toastmasters Convention.

I know this. Luckily for me, I take the stage first.

I'll take that as a compliment. Thank you. What's your topic?

Social Heredity - a concept coined by author Napoleon Hill in his book, Law of Success. Social Heredity represents the state of one's mind as a result of uninterrupted exposure to certain environmental conditions and influences. It's about the people, activities, challenges, and opportunities we're exposed to during our formative years. Unlike the Willie Lynch Syndrome, which is intended to enslave the human mind, Social Heredity can either build up or break down the mind, depending on the environmental conditions and influences.

Now, that's a twist. I haven't spoken about the Willie Lynch Syndrome publicly in years. However, this concept of Social Heredity is definitely something I'd like to explore further.

I'm cool with that. I noticed many scripture references in your book. I didn't realize the Bible had so much to teach us about money. Where did you learn this?

Last year we decided our children should be exposed to biblical principles and other positive influences. After some research, I discovered Crown Financial Ministries. During a conversation with a fellow Toastmaster, I mentioned Crown and he told me that his church offered the course. We attended a few services and thoroughly enjoyed the experience. The children's ministry and youth entrepreneur program gave us the incentive to join. I'm currently leading a Crown Small Group study on Monday nights.

I think I've heard of Crown. What did you gain from the study?

>The most important principle is that everything belongs to God, but is entrusted to man. The second principle is based on Proverbs 13:22 which states, "A good man leaves an inheritance for his children's children." In essence, our actions today should make life more enjoyable and less complicated for our grandchildren.

That's it! Proverbs 13:22 is the principle I've been searching for.

>What do you mean?

I'm not exactly sure, but it has something to do with our motivation for coming together. How does Proverbs 13:22 apply to <u>My Money Works For Me</u>?

>Everyone has a genius within, which by some extraordinary power can pave the way to exceptional health, abundant wealth, and never-ending fulfillment. My responsibility as a teacher is to educate parents and children on how to achieve the financial aspect of Proverbs 13:22. I'm currently using a game called Cashflow 101 to accomplish this goal.

A game, hmmm! Did you create this game?

>No, I didn't. A real estate guru named Robert Kiyosaki created the game in 1996. He has a book titled <u>Rich Dad Poor Dad</u> which shares the story leading to the creation of Cashflow 101.

What kind of results are you getting from the game?

>The results are phenomenal for the people who are committed to the program. What's really cool is watching the light bulb turn on when a person realizes how simple it is to play the game of money and win.

I think you've nailed it, Jackson. Listen, I would love to continue this conversation, but I have a doctor's appointment in thirty minutes. Are you available to meet this evening around 7:00pm?

>Sure! Where do you want to meet?

How about the Barnes and Noble on Pleasant Hill?

Works for me. I'll see you at seven.

On the way to his appointment, Psoloman received a call from his book agent Kenyette Maxwell. She informed him about the publishing deal she'd been negotiating and suggested they meet at 7:00pm to celebrate and go over the details. Psoloman agreed, but changed the time to 6:00pm.

They met at Barnes and Noble. The book publishing deal satisfied Psoloman's requirements, and he told Kenyette to move forward.

Jackson arrived shortly before 7:00pm. Psoloman introduced Jackson to Kenyette, and she recognized him from the picture in his book. Kenyette asked Jackson a few questions and then excused herself. For the next two hours, Jackson and Psoloman discussed the core principles presented in their respective books, particularly Proverbs 13:22. Jackson brought a few copies of the financial worksheet and showed Psoloman how the numbers flow. He also invited Psoloman to Cashflow 101 Game Night on Tuesday. Psoloman gladly accepted.

Chapter 32

A Call For Teachers

Psoloman's Moment of Truth

To prepare for the big event, the newlyweds spent the day at the spa. Psoloman adores Antoinette. Her attention to detail has provided him the greatest benefit a man could receive from a woman – her support. Antoinette's love for Psoloman is intense and unrestrained. In her arms, he feels safe, relaxed, and appreciated.

They arrived at the Atlanta Marriot Marquis at 4:00pm to set up his product and information table in the hotel lobby. After setting up the table, Psoloman took a walk into the conference hall and then across the stage to the lectern. He visualized himself delivering a phenomenal keynote address and winning over the hearts of hundreds of communicators and leaders.

As Antoinette entered the conference hall, her phone rang. It was Psoloman letting her know he was headed to the hotel room to review his notes. She said, "I love you," and headed to the bar to get a drink.

Smiling, the bartender said to her, "What can I get for you, pretty lady?' Antoinette responded, "I'll have a sprite. Better yet, make it a root beer." "Are you sure?" replied the bartender. "Yes, I'm sure," she said.

While the bartender was making her drink, Antoinette scoped the room to see who she would meet today. Connecting with people was her greatest strength. She spotted Jackson Gray, recognizing him from the photo in the book he'd sent to Psoloman.

The bartender handed her the root beer, and she walked over to the table to introduce herself. "Hi, I'm Antoinette. Do you mind if I join you?" Jackson responded, "Absolutely! By the way, my name is Jackson Gray and this is my wife Geovana, my cousin Shari, my best friend Lawrence, and his wife Pam. Are you here alone or should we pull up another chair?" Antoinette responded, "One chair is fine.   I'm here with my husband Psoloman Blacksmith. He's upstairs preparing for his speech." "When did the two of you tie the knot, Jackson questioned." "We had a private ceremony two weeks ago."

The group shared comments about marriage, honeymoons, and children for thirty minutes and then began making their way to the conference hall to locate their table. After seating Geovana, Jackson joined Psoloman at the speaker's table. It was strategically located to minimize travel time of the presenters to the stage. The ladies continued the conversation they began at the bar.

At 6:00pm sharp, the ceremony began with the Pledge of Allegiance and Invocation. The incoming Toastmasters International President, Ted Corcoran, provided opening words of encouragement and conducted the awards ceremony. Following the awards ceremony, he delivered a superb introduction for the Toastmaster of the evening and welcomed him to the stage.

As Toastmaster for the 2003 Annual Toastmasters International Convention, please help me welcome to the stage my friend and mentor, Atlanta's own Mr. Everett McNish.

The crowd cheered as Everett made his way to the stage. He moved like a man on a mission – filled with excitement and that warm smile many Toastmasters have come to love.

Everett's ability to persuade and command an audience is second to none. In fact, Psoloman spent the past year learning from Everett, who was delighted to see one of his students take the stage as keynote speaker.

Immediately following the Golden Gavel Award, presented to Mrs. Debbie Fields, Kene introduced Psoloman.

Toastmasters from around the world, Mayor Shirley Franklin, Governor Sonny Perdue, incoming Toastmasters International President Ted Corcoran, Ladies and Gentlemen and tonight in particular, Mr. Psoloman Blacksmith:

You're in for a treat this evening. I've had the pleasure of working with and learning from this young man during the last twelve months. He has an unparalleled passion and commitment to unite people from around the world. His mission is to equip us to build quality relationships in our homes and create healthy learning environments for our children.

Psoloman's speech is titled, "A Call For Teachers." Please help me welcome to the stage, with a level of enthusiasm that can be heard and felt in California, our keynote speaker – Mr. Psoloman Blacksmith.

Psoloman moved swiftly to the stage. A key factor in his presentation was to draw the attention of the crowd immediately, by injecting into their hearts his own enthusiasm. Psoloman shook hands with Everett, gave him a hug, and jumped right into the speech.

Imagine This...

Men and Women, the young and the mature - skin tones in varying shades of black, brown, red, yellow and white - sitting peacefully at a round table having a stimulating, yet purposeful discussion about our children, about our relationships, about the way we think, decide, and live.

I know this may seem far-fetched, but can you please, just for the moment, set aside your preferences and entertain (in spite of the opposing viewpoints) this discussion which I have imagined?

Let us come together. The influential Christian pastor and the misguided young man or woman.

Let us come together. The audaciously innovative teacher and the bored, yet intelligent student.

Let us come together. The relentlessly loving mother and the still innocent kid who is attracted to a life of crime.

Let us come together. The outstanding citizens from cultures around the world and the mishandled, mistreated, and misled . . . *they've suffered enough.*

Mr. Toastmaster, Fellow Toastmasters, Distinguished and Honored Guests, tonight I will present a grand problem for us to solve collectively. This problem is too big for me to tackle alone. However, if we join together, uniting under the guidelines that I will present tonight, our relationships will blossom and solutions will begin to magically unfold.

Before I continue, may I ask you an important series of questions about human relationships?

Where would you be sitting and next to whom, had your seats not been pre-assigned? Would it be the person to your left and right? Would the arrangement of people reflect the diversity in skin tone, nationality, age and sex, which I see from this stage? Or would we be arranged in packs like animals, isolated from those who differ in some way?

Your answer to these questions is important, as it relates to today's presentation – A Call For Teachers. Please relax and realize that I come not to condemn you, but to confirm what my research has led me to know and understand.

It's been made clear to me that a great opportunity stands before us if we will just open our eyes, open our minds, and open our hearts to the idea that much of what we have learned about people is untrue. In fact, if each of you would honestly evaluate the ideas you embrace, I'm positive you will discover that most of what you know is based on what someone else believed to be true.

A large percentage of the ideas on which many of us base our decisions have been handed down to us by the teachers and key influencers of our formative years. Let me suggest that until you've labored to gain your own understanding about your fears, desires, and experiences, you're missing an important piece of who you are and what you're capable of contributing to society. I come forth boldly tonight to say that your best life cannot and will not be lived until you gain the confidence to question, analyze, and validate everything you believe about yourself and others.

This self-study should help you answer two questions and initiate the relationship healing process which I will cover shortly. The first question is: What makes you unique and brilliant? The second question is just as important. How can you share your uniqueness and brilliance with others, to increase their value and make their lives more enjoyable? These questions are tied directly to the greatest commandments ever presented to man.

The Bible teaches us in the book of Matthew chapter 22, beginning at verse 34, God desires for us to first love Him, with all we have to give – heart, soul, and mind. I believe God wants us to focus our love and attention exclusively on Him, so that He may begin teaching us how to love ourselves and in-turn, love our black, brown, red, yellow, and white neighbors. Are you still with me?

Today I ask you, put away the desire to point out and demonstrate how or why we differ in theology, philosophy and culture.   Instead, let's seek SOMETHING which engages minds, uplifts spirits, and equips men, women, and children to succeed in their endeavors.   It's time for us to give birth to a new institution of learning - one which fully prepares the student for the future undertaking.

Many of the current institutions have failed us and continue to fail us. Instead of teaching us how to interact with and bring value to one another, the knowledge we have gained frequently leads to divorce, domestic violence, teenage pregnancy, drug addiction, religious cult affiliation, incarceration, slavery to debt, poor communication, and worst of all, fear and presumption.   We are literally afraid of one another, because we lack the courage to challenge our own prejudices. This must stop today!

Ralph Waldo Emerson taught us that, "The ancestor of every action is a thought." What we must do through a new institution of learning is reprogram the mind with a knowledge that cultivates *a thinking man and woman!* Without thinkers, we become slaves to the problems which plague society. Thinkers point out better options and help us deliver attractive results. The Bible puts it this way: "As a man thinketh in his heart, so is he."

Now, what do I profess to be a more attractive result? My friend Jackson Gray, a phenomenal speaker whom you don't want to miss during tonight's schedule of events, provided this answer: "*A good man leaves an inheritance [of moral stability and goodness] to his children's children.*"

How do we become the catalyst which triggers a series of conversations and actions that lead to families and communities getting better and better with each year? How do we become the model for cultivating quality relationships which restore trust and demonstrate the power of leadership and teamwork?

We begin considering the possibility that what we currently know is not enough. Albert Einstein taught us that, "*We cannot solve our problems with the same thinking we used when we created them.*"

Next, we vacate methods of instruction which have proven to be unfruitful. Albert Toffler taught us that, "*The illiterate of the 21st century will not be those who cannot read and write, but those who cannot learn, unlearn, and relearn.*"

Finally, we commit to making decisions that build bridges instead of dams - decisions which promote, encourage, and inspire new life in others. This insight is organized and packaged in the bestselling book of all time – The Bible, also known as the book of life.

LIFE is the common thread that clothes us. LIFE is the unifying force that ignites in all human beings, a burning desire to contribute something significant. We gain access to an abundant and fulfilling LIFE when act wisely, motivated by love rather than fear; motivated by God rather than personal success and suffering.

It's time to decide. Are you fed up with broken families and dysfunctional communities? If yes, let's agree to do what is necessary to leave an inheritance for our children's children.

This is not a sermon. It is a call for teachers. However, before we can be teachers, we must become students again. We must unlearn and relearn. We must reprogram our minds with God's thought system of love and wisdom. We must be the tree which bears the sweetest and the most desirable fruit – the tree of LIFE.

Tonight I offer you a new experience, a more attractive result – one which gives each of us more LIFE. However, I cannot accomplish this grand task alone. I need your help. Will you join me?

If your answer is yes, you'll find an envelope under your seat labeled "SIGN ME UP." The form takes less than three minutes to complete. Immediately following my presentation is a fifteen minute intermission, so you have plenty of time. Deliver your completed forms to the MWI Training Institute product and information table in the lobby. I will also be present to autograph copies of my book, Mixed Nuts.

As you complete your form and prepare for our next speaker, Jackson Gray, consider these words of wisdom. An institution of learning isn't worth a great deal if it teaches young people how to make a good living, but fails to prepare them to live an exceptional and rewarding life. Let's be the change we desire to see in the world.

Mr. Toastmaster.

Chapter 33

The Missing Ingredient

Kaiya and Tai Lynn Change The Game of Business

Sixty-four women. Fascinating. Beautiful. Quick-witted. Articulate. Penetrating. Distinct. Perceptive. Audacious. Nurturing. Unmatched. Intuitive. Thorough. Alert. Ultra precise. Powerful. Persuasive. Lovable. Tender. And Sexy.

Just a few adjectives to describe the women in my family away from home . . . *The Missing Ingredient, LLC.* Our fortune 500, world-class organization has redefined what it means to be a successful woman in today's business world. The organization consists of eight teams of eight women each (plus two, if you count Tai Lyn and me).

We've consistently helped businesses throughout the world deliver knock-your-socks-off service and generate record profits each month.

What's our secret? Balance! A balance between resources, time, and quality. Tai Lynn learned about creating a balanced organization during our college years at UGA. She participated in a series of case studies, which tested the principles presented in a business book titled <u>The Goal</u> by Dr. Eliyahu Goldratt.

Her team concluded: To achieve balance, you must be effective at serving the needs and employing the skills of your human resources – customers, employees, investors and suppliers. Every person who interacts with the organization is important to its success, and this interaction must be uncomplicated, systematic, and beneficial.

Our Strategic Coaching System places an emphasis on viable service as it relates to net profit. The measurements defined by our system determine the quality of service not only by net profit (money kept), but also by throughput (money in), inventory (money tied up), and operational expense (money out). Each of the measurements has something to do with money. In the end, net profit equals throughput minus operational expense.

By placing an emphasis on delivering a viable service to customers, employees, investors, and suppliers, most of our clients have been able to realize a steady increase in net profit from month-to-month. In fact, their retention rate of customers and employees has been significantly higher than their competitors. Suppliers have given them the best deals and fastest turn-around time and lenders have provided them the lowest rates on borrowed capital.

Before implementing our Strategic Coaching System, this level of success was considered highly unlikely. Relationships were, at best, obligatory rather than voluntary.

At The Missing Ingredient, LLC, we understand that relationships are the lifeblood of business performance and each relationship holds a key to delivering a viable service. When you truly know someone and understand their needs, you can position your organization to make their life less frustrating and oftentimes downright enjoyable. Relationships foster loyalty, trust, and respect, making way for giving people exactly what they want. We call it *The Quality Exchange*!

The first step in the Strategic Coaching System is to turn the client's business operation upside down. Instead of the CEO residing at the top of the organization, he or she is placed at the base. At the base, the CEO acts as the foundation or underlying strength for the entire organization. His or her leadership/service guides the decisions of each player on the team - decisions which ultimately solve problems or key frustrations for the organization's customers, employees, investors and suppliers. Could you imagine working for a company that operates in this manner? Or better yet, would you be interested in building an organization that operates as we've described? You could be our next client.

Now that I've piqued your interest, I will help you decide (in three easy steps) whether or not our services can meet your needs. Our ideal client is the CEO who understands the fundamentals of business, but lacks the strategy needed to improve the quality of service and increase net profit. Does this apply to your business? If it does, please continue reading.

The second step in the Strategic Coaching System is to nurture your decision-making skills in two areas: The first is effectively serving the needs and employing the skills of your human resources. The second is the proper use of time. Making quality decisions in both areas is the goal.

For clarification, let's define resources, time, and quality. Resources are the skills offered by your customers, employees, investors, and suppliers to improve and grow your organization. Time is the number of hours remaining before your resources leave you to invest in your competitor's organization. Quality is the current perceived value of your entire organization (and its viable solutions), as held in the minds of your customers, employees, investors, and suppliers.

Current Perceived Value is measured first in throughput (money in) and ultimately in net profit (money kept). Increased throughput tells you that your customers, employees, investors and suppliers are benefiting from the solutions offered by your organization. Increased net profit tells you the delivery system in your business is appropriate for satisfying the current market demand.

The third step in the Strategic Coaching System is to play a game. We want learning to be fun, engaging, instantly gratifying, and socially transforming. You'll meet other CEOs to share ideas and contacts, while developing your strategic thinking muscles. Take this insight back to your organization and revolutionize the way you do business.

In case you're wondering about the game, it's called Business Chess. It takes about one hour to play, depending on your skill level, using the same pieces as the standard chess game. A new set of rules have been designed to teach you how to serve the needs and employ the skills of your human resources.

Will you lose the game and go out of business due to a lack of focus, indecisiveness, poor planning and management, insufficient communication and execution, or failure to adapt to market changes? Don't try to answer this question without first putting your thinking to the test. We've already confirmed 6:30pm on Tuesday, October 7, 2003, with your administrative assistant. Please bring a guest. See you there.

Kaiya Sinclair

Jackson contacted Psoloman to attend the function as his guest. He also sent Kaiya an email to let her that Psoloman would be attending. Psoloman, excited by the power of the gaming experience, couldn't wait to attend the event.

Tai-Lynn Cho

Chapter 34

I Won't Let You Give Up On Your Dream!

When A Woman Loves A Man

Four years passed since his keynote address at the Toastmasters Conference. Depleted resources and ditched sponsorships left Psoloman frustrated and depressed. His vision inspired many to begin, but his leadership compelled them to quit.

Antoinette recognized Psoloman's weakness during the early stages and decided to do something to help. However, she kept it low-key to protect his pride and dignity. About a year after Psoloman launched his project, Antoinette began studying mastermind groups – a concept introduced by her college instructor, Professor Marcelle. Antoinette shared with him what she was trying to accomplish for Psoloman. Professor Marcelle suggested she read principle forty-six in The Success Principles by Jack Canfield, and then pulled the book from his library for Antoinette to review.

She opened the book and turned to the principle titled "Masterminding Your Way To Success." It read, "The basic philosophy of a mastermind group is that more can be achieved in less time when people work together. A mastermind group is made up of people who meet regularly - weekly, biweekly, or monthly - to share ideas, thoughts, information, feedback, and resources. By getting the perspective, knowledge, experience, and resources of the others in the group, not only can you move beyond your own limited view of the world, but you can also advance your own goals and projects more quickly."

Antoinette smiled and said, "Thank you Professor," and returned his book. She purchased a copy of The Success Principles on her way home. Three months later, Antoinette implemented Mr. Canfield's steps and established her first mastermind group. The mastermind group worked diligently on Project Psoloman for three years.

During this time, Psoloman's level of frustration increased, and he considered throwing in the towel. Antoinette continued to encourage him, knowing the efforts of her mastermind group were paying off. Psoloman unknowingly provided the expertise, while Antoinette relayed the information to her mastermind group, in order to give shape and definition to Psoloman's dream.

When the time was right, Antoinette set up a meeting with the business strategy coach in her mastermind group. At first, Psoloman resisted. However, Antoinette persuaded him to give it one more try when she told him the appointment was with Tai-Lynn Cho. Psoloman remembered her from the business chess event he'd attended with Jackson. Excited by the opportunity, Psoloman began asking Antoinette questions about Tai Lynn. He wanted to know how she'd met Tai Lynn. Antoinette played dumb and told Psoloman that Professor Marcelle made the recommendation. He knew Antoinette wasn't telling him everything, but decided to go with the flow and attend the meeting, scheduled for 2:00pm the following day.

While sleeping, Psoloman had a vision. He was back at the Toastmasters meeting, listening to Jackson's speech "We Are Worthy of Respect and Admiration." Only this time, he wasn't offended. His journal was filled with notes from previous conversations with Jackson. Each journal entry was dated and summarized the key points of each discussion, twenty-four in all. The first entry was made on 05/09/94. Psoloman was puzzled by the date, since his first meeting with Jackson didn't take place until January 2000.

Antoinette woke up at 3:00am to find Psoloman sitting at the kitchen table. He had eight Bibles, in different translations, opened to First Corinthians 12. She asked, "What are you doing, sweetheart?" He responded, "I had this vision while I was sleeping, and I'm trying to figure out what the numbers mean – 5, 9, 9 and 4. Antoinette suggested he sleep on it. Psoloman agreed. He continued to think about the numbers until drifting off to sleep.

Professor Marcelle

Chapter 35

Tower Place

The Most Prestigious Business Address in Atlanta

Hello, Cindy. My name is Psoloman Blacksmith. I have a two o'clock appointment with Mrs. Tai Lynn Cho.

> Yes, Mr. Blacksmith, she is expecting you. Can I get you something to drink?

No thank you, Cindy.

> OK. Please have a seat and Mrs. Cho will be with you shortly.

Psoloman picked up a magazine. On the cover was none other than Tai-Lynn Cho and Kaiya Sinclair Yuma — 2006 Businesswomen of the Year. The article shared the vision of their company - The Missing Ingredient, LLC, as well as testimonials from many of their satisfied clients.

He put the magazine down and thought back to his vision. Still, Psoloman couldn't make sense of the numbers. Then it hit him, "Jackson's release date from Reidsville!" He stood, as if this were some great discovery, before returning to his seat. Soon after, a petite, yet stunningly attractive Asian woman extended her hand.

Mr. Blacksmith, it's such a pleasure to meet you. I've been waiting over three years and I'm excited!

> Three Years?

Yes! Antoinette has been working with Kaiya and me for the last thirty-six months. When Antoinette came into my office and presented your ideas, we fell in love with your vision. Today, it has come to life, and we want to present to you the proposed solution.

> Ohhhhhh . . . Kay. Well, where do we start?

We've put together a ten minute DVD presentation highlighting the ideas you've uncovered through your research. What you've done is amazing! You're really going to enjoy this.

Psoloman watched in awe the multimedia presentation and 3D model of POISE University - *a two year university built upon his research*. Part two of the presentation highlighted their board game – Life$TYLE Harmony - designed to teach the core principles in a fun, yet challenging way.

> Wow!   You guys have been busy.   Antoinette facilitated this project?

She sure did! Antoinette has been observing your genius very closely and taking notes. We've met every Tuesday night during the last three years. I'm sure she told you about her mastermind group project. And don't be concerned with the legal aspects of protecting your work; she covered you in that area too. You should be proud of her.

> I'm very proud of Antoinette. Can you give me a minute to call and thank her?

Why don't you do it in person? Antoinette, you can come out now. I'd also like you to meet the rest of the team – the people who know you intimately and care about this vision as much as you do.

To his surprise, all of his friends followed Antoinette into the conference room - Jackson and Geovana Gray, Dr. Yuma and his wife Kaiya, and finally Professor Marcelle – also known as "Coach M" by the team.

Professor Marcelle was the first person to join with Antoinette. His extensive background in leadership and teamwork provided the insight she needed to select the right members. Overwhelmed with excitement and gratitude, Psoloman looked up and said, "Thank you, Father." He greeted and thanked the team. They spent the rest of the afternoon playing Life$TYLE Harmony and discussing the curriculum for POISE University.

Chapter 36

The Invitation

Game Board Preview

Lawrence Alexander

From:	GeoThePoet@yahoo.com
Sent:	Saturday, February 23, 2008 9:15 AM
To:	CF101 Facilitators; Life$TYLE Project Team; Life$TYLE Guests
Subject:	Life$TYLE Harmony Board Game Launch – March 8th

The Life$TYLE Harmony Board Game launch is coming up in a few weeks on Saturday, March 8, 2008, at 9:00am. We'll be meeting at The Missing Ingredient, LLC, in Atlanta. Breakfast will be served at 8:00am.

The address is:

> The Missing Ingredient, LLC
> Tower Place
> 3340 Peachtree Road, Suite 1801
> Atlanta, GA 30326

We'll have thirty game boards to accommodate everyone; five are reserved for single men and women, five for middle-aged couples, five for senior couples, five for newlyweds, and the remaining ten for trainers, entrepreneurs, administrators, and ministers. Seating has been assigned based on your Life$TYLE Preferences Questionnaire. This is done to ensure you'll have common interests and aspirations with the other five players at your game table.

For those interested, you'll have the option to continue playing Life$TYLE Harmony with your assigned group and receive specialized life skills training for twenty-six weeks. The training fee will be waived for all students who attend the Life$TYLE Harmony Board Game Launch on March 8th. However, you must commit to attending and participating in the twenty-six week Life$TYLE Training Program. Additional information will be provided to you on Saturday.

When you arrive at Tower Place, look for the signs to direct you to the large conference room. If you have any questions, a representative will be at the front door to assist you. Thank you for your participation and support. I'll see you on game day.

Geovana Gray

Chapter 37

Sincere Appreciation

Psoloman's Conversation With God

Good morning, God. I've been thinking about some things lately. I just want to speak with you before I head out to the Life$TYLE Harmony Board Game launch. Thank you for allowing me to remain a contributor to this vision. I haven't done so well with the many people who've been sent to assist me. I'm still struggling to understand why I couldn't make the proper adjustments in my dealings with others.

> Your mind has planned the way, but it is my responsibility to direct your steps and make them sure. Son, there are many things which you have learned; so much that I have taught you. However, you have not learned everything. This makes it important for you to remain in continuous dialogue with Me during all stages of your affairs. Think of me as your football coach and yourself as the quarterback. I call the plays and you help the team execute each play successfully.

I've never looked at things that way. I felt silly seeking Your insight when I already had an answer. Are you telling me that You want to be consulted on every step, no matter how simple it may seem?

> Absolutely, Psoloman! It is easy for man to be deceived and led astray; even he who is dedicated to do something worthwhile. And do not believe for a second that someone else is responsible. If you are deceived, your thinking is the root of the deception. Satan, as many people call him, is only as powerful as you allow him to be in your life. His role is to test your understanding of My principles and help you see what you still need to learn. It is okay for you to slip once. However, to ignore the fact that you are slipping tells Me that you are being guided by your own foolish ways. Continuous dialogue with Me is the key to getting what you want in life.

You're speaking of my leadership skills. Although I was exposed to leadership principles in Professor Marcelle's study group, I failed to practice what I had learned.   The Law of Process, The Law of Navigation, The Law of the Inner Circle, and The Law of Victory.   I was so busy working on the vision that I forgot to work on myself.

> Many of My students have engaged the pursuit unwisely. It is part of the learning process. What you must decide today is how long will you continue being an ineffective leader? I certainly can choose someone else to bring forth the vision which I have planted in you.

Please don't take this away from me, God. Tell me what I must do to increase my effectiveness with Your people.

> You must do exactly as I instructed Joshua – purposefully study My wisdom day and night; meditate upon it continuously, engage Me in conversation frequently, and expect Me to show you what to do next. Since you're studying leadership and I've already raised an exceptional teacher of leadership principle, you must allow him to be your mentor. He will not mentor you personally at this stage; however, his books and audio lessons are sufficient.   Jackson presented this source to you eight years ago, but you weren't ready. The 21 Most Powerful Minutes of A Leader's Day will be your best friend during the next six months. Keep it at your side and study it frequently. More importantly, do what it says.

But what if I don't understand something?

> Son, your success is up to you. If you allow your mind to think continuously of failure and misunderstanding, you will create an environment which allows failure and misunderstanding to come to your doorstep. Think only about the results you intend to create; then consult with Me for the plan of action.

Okay, God. Thanks again for keeping me on the team. Thank you for bringing Antoinette into my life. Thank you for making my dreams a reality. Finally, I ask that all of our guests and team members arrive safely and with their best thinking. Allow the Life$TYLE Harmony

Board Game launch to be a huge success and a key factor in the evolution of human relationship and education. I love you, Father!

Chapter 38

Home Life Says It All

How One Man Became A Better Father and Husband

Practical Insight To Increase Your Net Profit

MONDAY, December 1, 2008

Family Is The Name of This Game

I had the most amazing experience two Sundays ago. What do say about a seemingly insignificant board game that totally changes people lives? You know, board games, like Monopoly, Sorry, Chess, Backgammon, Scrabble, and The Game of Life. This game is the ultimate emotional charge – *fierce competition, major setbacks, piercing questions that make you say why did I land of that space?* It also transforms you into an intellectual powerhouse through group discussion, personality insight, and sharing your if-only-I-could-find-a-way-to-pursue-my dreams with supportive people. You walk away excited with possibility. Doesn't this make you tingle inside? Doesn't it make you want to play the game, just once?

We interviewed the Life$TYLE Harmony Game design team last week at Mrs. Gray's house, mother of game designer and author Jackson Gray. They meet every week for a three-hour game, followed by Sunday dinner. Jennifer Wallace, Matthew Swanson, and I participated in their Life$TYLE Harmony Game session to get a real hands-on experience from the pros. There were eight Life$TYLE Harmony Game sessions with four players per table. Matthew, Jennifer, and I played at different tables and later discussed what we'd learned. We've never been challenged with the types of questions and scenarios presented during the game. It was strikingly engaging - an awesome and unforgettable learning experience.

One of the players had this to say about his experience. "Life$TYLE Harmony has not only improved the quality of my business performance and profits, but has also improved the quality of my relationships at home with my wife and children. My wife frequently tells me how patient I've become. She also appreciates that I now solicit her input when making major decisions which impact our family. Before learning the principles taught in the Life$TYLE Harmony Game, I'd just do whatever I felt appropriate. Today, leadership and teamwork are the significant factors governing our family's decision-making process. My wife and I work together like teammates. Best of all, my 15-year-old daughter said to me the other day, *'Dad, I really like you now.'* Then she gave me a big hug. It's been the highlight of my year."

Life$TYLE Harmony: *The Game of Building Quality Relationships In Order To Create Wealth and Enjoy Life* has been a hot ticket item since its release on May 1, 2008. The players interviewed for our case study have been playing the game weekly with the designers since its inception.

I sat at the table with Tai Lynn Cho and Kaiya Sinclair-Yuma, 2006 Businesswomen of the Year, who released their new book Freedom Is The Goal last month. They are responsible for the strategic decision-making component of the Life$TYLE Harmony Game. Tai Lynn shared these words with me:

"Life$TYLE will revolutionize the quality and frequency of your interactions with family, friends, and business affiliates. The emphasis placed on building life-giving relationships and making superb decisions has positioned the Life$TYLE Harmony Game to be the preferred source of instruction among trainers, entrepreneurs, administrators, and even ministers. If you want to create loyal customers and build profits, improve your relationships, or sharpen your decision-making skills, the Life$TYLE

Harmony Game is simply the best educational tool on the market today. It's fun, simple, and it works!"

My recommendation to every small business owner, leader, teacher, and parent is to play the Life$TYLE Harmony Game as soon as possible. If you're stimulated by the experience, join one of the Life$TYLE Harmony Mastermind Groups. I'm positive that playing the Life$TYLE Harmony Game regularly will totally change the way you think about and approach your life and business affairs. It has changed my life, and I'm looking forward to the first game session with my Life$TYLE Harmony Mastermind group.

Visit www.LifestyleHarmonyGame.com to sign up for your FREE LifeSTYLE Harmony Game session. Sessions are currently being facilitated every Saturday from 1:00pm to 5:00pm. The locations are listed on the website.

Kennedy Anderson
The Business Blogger

Chapter 39

The Calm Before The Storm

Psoloman Gets Blindsided By Love

It's been fifteen months since the release of the Life$TYLE Harmony Game. Tai Lynn and Kaiya's book <u>Freedom Is The Goal</u> has been a top seller for the past twenty-nine weeks. Not only have they negotiated a publishing agreement to release her book in Japanese and Spanish, but they have also tripled their number of clients, booked four sold out strategic coaching conferences, and expanded to an international office in Nagoya, Japan.

BusinessWeek Magazine rated <u>LifestyleHarmonyGame.com</u> as the number one training and development portal for small business owners in America. Customer feedback, game board sales, and attendance at monthly conferences confirm Life$TYLE has delivered on its promise to make us better decision makers. Teachers, entrepreneurs, administrators, and ministers travel to Atlanta from various cities each month to test their skills, share leadership and life principles, and learn profit-generation strategies.

In an effort to implement a Life$TYLE Harmony Game training program in public schools, the team began carefully reviewing customer feedback. Ninety-two customers, mostly teachers, expressed an interest in teaching the Life$TYLE Harmony Game to teenagers, especially those raised in a single parent household. After several meetings with the team, Antoinette arranged a conference with a group of sixty-three teachers, entrepreneurs, administrators, and ministers to discuss the opportunity. Mindbuilders™ – *a state-of-the-art library and personal growth center* – was launched. Antoinette's interpersonal skills attracted the labor and resources of thousands of volunteers and sponsors; she quickly raised the $9.5 million required to build the facility.

Targeted to open in Fall 2011, The Mindbuilders™ Project has required everyone's participation and expertise. Eighty students have completed the pilot program for Mindbuilders™ Level 1 training, which teaches leadership, finance, and communication skills. The training recently proved beneficial as parents began to notice and report significant changes in their children's grades and behavior.

In addition to her contribution to Mindbuilders™, Geovana partnered with Katrina Vascuez to launch a series of seminars for young women and teenage mothers. The seminars focus on four areas: *Communication, Administration, Leadership, and Home Economics.* The first seminar was conducted two months ago on June 8, 2009 and there was a huge turnout. Many of the seminar participants received promotions or acquired better jobs as a result of completing the training and applying what they'd learned. The home economics program has been a favorite, teaching mothers how to care for their children and create a warm, nurturing environment in their homes.

Katrina's Virtuous Woman Program is being expanded for Mindbuilders™. She and Dr. Yuma are developing a training system based on the Women's Study Bible, published by Thomas Nelson. The goal is to create a place for women to learn from and encourage one another, using biblical principles as a guideline.

Dr. Yuma's team is brainstorming a couples training system called The Intimate Partners Club. He hopes to use internet technology, web-based training, board game driven social events, and retreats to facilitate the training. The ultimate goal is to make information available to couples when they need it so that better decisions can be made to protect the marriage. Once approved, they'll begin developing The Intimate Partners Club Project over the next three years, making it available for couples Fall\Winter 2012.

Kaiya and Psoloman joined forces and published <u>90 Day Roadmap To Job</u> <u>Success</u>. They share ninety ways to increase your value in the workplace and earn the highest salary supported by the employer. The book also introduces the C.O.R.E. Skill Development Plan and Goal Setting Strategy.

C.O.R.E. stands for **C**ompensation, **O**pportunities, **R**esources, and **E**xperts. Psoloman and Kaiya have invested many hours developing and promoting C.O.R.E. training. Book signings, seminars, and business meetings have been scheduled in fifty U.S. cities. Several Atlanta-based businesses have implemented C.O.R.E. and experienced an increase in employee morale, productivity, and net profit. Psoloman and Kaiya have begun building a network of C.O.R.E. facilitators to accelerate their progress and multiply the results.

In spite of his phenomenal success, Psoloman continues to train with the intensity and discipline of an Olympic gold medalist. His daily workout includes three hours of bible study, which always precedes his other activities, two hours of research for his current project, followed by three hours of product development, usually writing. He practices this standard Monday, Wednesday, and Friday, leaving Tuesday and Thursday open for meetings and personal restoration activities. Tuesday and Thursday are also dating nights for him and Antoinette. Saturday is reserved for Ana Elyse, their five-year-old daughter. She decides the activities for the day and nothing takes precedence. On Sunday, they attend the 1:00pm church service at 12Stone and then head to Mrs. Gray's for Sunday dinner and the Life$TYLE Harmony Game.

Psoloman was preparing for a C.O.R.E. seminar when he received the emergency call from his mom. The ringtone let him know who was calling, but he still let the call go to voicemail. Psoloman typically didn't take calls while working, unless it was Antoinette. Then his phone beeped a second time indicating a new text message. It read, "Urgent! Please call me right away. Mom."

404-532-9163

Hey, Mom! Are you okay?

> Hi, baby. I'm fine, but we need to talk. Are you going Sunday dinner tonight at Mrs. Gray's?

I am. Why? What's up?

> I know you're probably getting ready for church, and I hate to interrupt, but can you meet me at her house in forty-five minutes?

Meet you there? Why do you want to meet me at Mrs. Gray's? You'll pass right by my house on the way.

> I know. It's a long story, son. Just make sure you're there and please come alone. It's about time you found out the truth.

The truth about what?

> I'll tell you when I get there.

Antoinette and Ana Elyse were just walking into the house. They'd stopped at the bakery to pick up a cake for Sunday dinner. When she saw the puzzled look on Psoloman's face, Antoinette placed the cake on the table and asked, "Honey, what's wrong?" Psoloman responded, "Mom called and said that it's time I learned the truth." "The truth about what," Antoinette asked. Psoloman hesitated before responding, "I don't know. It kind of has me worried. Mom doesn't handle things this way. She's very structured and disciplined. She asked me to come alone. Are you okay with that?" Antoinette responded with concern, "Sure! But call me *as soon as* you find out what's going on." "Okay, sweetheart! I'll be back to for you and Ana Elyse," he replied. "Love you," she said. "Love you too, baby," he said and kissed her passionately.

Ana Elyse, giggling asked, "What about me, daddy?" "I could never forget about you, pumpkin," Psoloman replied. He kneeled down and she jumped into his arms. For a moment, he forgot about the call from his mom. Then he told Ana Elyse, "Daddy has to go and meet JuJu. I'll see you in a little while." "Okay, daddy. I love you." "I love you too, pumpkin." Psoloman grabbed his keys and headed out. His phone rang as he backed on the street. It was Jackson.

Chapter 40

Julianne Blacksmith-Jones

A Decision She Doesn't Regret

Julianne's usual smile was absent, replaced by worry and uncertainty. Mrs. Gray greeted her at the door and then invited Julianne into the kitchen. Jackson questioned, "Mom, what's going on?" Mrs. Gray responded, "Please give us a few minutes." Psoloman knocked on the door as they disappeared into the kitchen.

In the kitchen, Mrs. Gray continued preparing dinner while she listened to Julianne share what the two of them knew would eventually surface. Julianne asked for her advice and then listened attentively. With a kind and gentle tone, Mrs. Gray said, "This matter is not about your career; rather it's a matter of doing what's right. For years, we've concealed the truth from our sons. Now the day has come for us to reveal the truth. If it's okay with you, I think it would be best for you to lead the conversation. Do you agree?" Julianne responded, "I think you're right." Mrs. Gray smiled and said, "You need a drink." Julianne replied, "Yes, a glass of wine would be nice."

Julianne and Mrs. Gray remained in the kitchen for about twenty minutes before returning to the living room. Julianne took a chair from the dining room table and placed it in front of Jackson and Psoloman. She took their hands and said, "I'm so sorry. I've been dreading this day for a long time, wondering how I would tell the two of you about your father, Spencer Dwayne Gray."

With a shocked expression on his face, Psoloman turned to Jackson, and then to his mom and said, "What the fuck, Mom?" Mrs. Gray interjected, "Boy, have you lost your damn mind? She's still your mother. Use another disrespectful word and you'll have to deal with me. Understood?" He replied, "Yes, ma'am!"

Julianne continued, "I realize that I've lied to you, but I only did it for your protection. You have no idea what challenges you've been able to avoid simply because people think you are white. Black men don't have it easy in this country." Jackson inserted, "You've got that right!" Julianne continued, "Statistics prove that a black man has to be twice as good at everything, just to be considered. As your mother, I couldn't let you go through it. So I lied. The only reason that I'm telling you now is because the newspapers and TV stations plan to run a story tomorrow about Spencer and I'd rather tell you myself."

Jackson embraced Psoloman and suggested, "Your mom has a point. I don't totally agree with her reasoning, but I think I understand. Show your mom some love, bro."

Feeling betrayed, Psoloman went out on the front porch to get some fresh air. Countless memories and questions flooded his mind, as he sat with his back to the wall.

Jackson knew exactly what Psoloman needed. He called Geovana and asked her to pick up Antoinette and Ana Elyse. When they arrived, Antoinette moved quickly to Psoloman's side to comfort him. Jackson filled Geovana in on the details, and she just smiled. Then Psoloman came inside, gave his mom a hug, and said, "Thank you, Mom. I love you too."

Mrs. Gray rang the kitchen bell and everyone sat down for Sunday dinner. They skipped the Life$TYLE Harmony game session and talked instead about the importance of the family sticking together in times of trouble. The evening turned out to be a joyous occasion.

On August 3, 2009, the article about the scandal hit the newsstands. Fulton County District Attorney Victoria Sax and Metro Police Chief Ronald Stewart announced the indictment of former Atlanta Police Chief Jerome Barrett in connection with the February 1972 homicide of Officer Spencer Dwayne Gray. Though Julianne was not connected to the murder, the article mentioned her relationship with Spencer, exposing the pregnancy and information about Psoloman's life and career. The investigation of the thirty-seven-year-old murder case was led by Spencer's ex-partner and best friend, Detective James Kendrick.

As a result of the investigation, several sponsors broke ties with Psoloman. However, their decision to withdraw did not hurt sales. 90 Day Roadmap To Job Success sold one hundred thousand units during the week following Psoloman's C.O.R.E. seminar in Chicago. Within six months, Life$TYLE Harmony Game sales reached five hundred thousand units. Antoinette began negotiations with several high schools, public and private, to incorporate Life$TYLE Harmony Training as an elective for sophomores, juniors, and seniors. Psoloman and Jackson partnered with leaders at Psoloman's church, World Changers International, to create a Life$TYLE Harmony Training Program to address the problems of poor money management and declining relationships within the church.

Chapter 41

Helping A Friend In Need

Jackson Learns An Important Lesson About Commitment

Bernadette Richardson arrived at Reidsville Georgia State Prison one hour before visitation. This was an important step in her routine. The four-hour drive from Atlanta had always been difficult for her emotionally. Bernadette visited Clyde every Saturday, and had done so for the last twenty-nine years.

After parking the car, she'd say a prayer. It was always the same prayer, "God, please forgive me for what I've done." Then she'd roll down the windows, light up a cigarette, pull out a picture of her and Clyde immaculately dressed, and think about the way they used to dance. Bernadette absolutely loved dancing with Clyde, particularly to Latin music. They used to compete in dance contests, not so much for the prize money, but for the ultimate satisfaction they experienced on the dance floor. Some of their most intimate moments happened while they danced together.

At the tender age of seven, Bernadette began taking dance lessons. She was passionate about style, flair, and pizzazz, whenever she stepped onto the dance floor. Clyde wasn't as passionate about dancing, but he certainly was intoxicated by Bernadette's charm, sex appeal, beauty, and love for the art. He thoroughly enjoyed being close to her – touching her skin, hearing her voice, and watching her smile. He'd carefully observe and study Bernadette, fascinated by the details which made her uniquely brilliant and attractive. These memories comforted Bernadette and, though they could not replace Clyde, they did provide her a healthy escape from the lifestyle she'd cultivated to cope with the pain and loneliness she felt.

Bernadette had recently quit drinking, a habit she picked up shortly after Clyde's trial. Although Clyde had willingly pled guilty to the murder, she knew he would've chosen differently had all the facts been presented.

Withholding these facts had cost Bernadette a fortune – a life of deep regret, loneliness, and self-condemnation.

After reminiscing about the times when Clyde was free, and she was happiest, Bernadette would play Minnie Ripperton's <u>Loving You</u>, pretending that Clyde was listening. The song reminded her of the first time she made love to Clyde, and it expressed in exact terms how she'd give anything to wake up in his arms again. Then she'd cry until there were no more tears, pull herself together, and head into the building to see her husband.

Preoccupied with a problem she'd been addressing, Bernadette's usual excitement was absent as she greeted Clyde. He knew something was on her mind, but decided not to press the issue. Instead, Clyde took her hand, looked into her eyes and smiled. The pain she'd quietly communicated during her last two visits had intensified, deepened and escalated beyond her control. Her smile had taken residence somewhere between Atlanta and Reidsville, and Clyde knew he'd have to address the issue with a quiet, yet intense resolve.

Baby, would you like to talk about it?

    Clyde, I've lied to you.

What are you talking about?

    I had an affair.

Recently?

    No. Twenty-nine years ago.

What are you trying to say Bernadette?

    The police officer.

The police officer that I found dead in my living room?

    Yes.

No. You can't be serious?

It's true.

So you're telling me that I've spent the last twenty-nine years of my life, dying a little each day, in a place not fit even for rats, because of your shallowness, your selfish desires, your stupidity? You insensitive, inconsiderate . . . I can't believe what I'm hearing!

Clyde, I'm sorry. Your work seemed to be the only thing that mattered. You had neglected me for so long. I needed someone to hold me, to touch me, to make love to me.

After realizing my mistake, I tried to break things off with him, but he wouldn't leave me alone. I was so used to you and I being together, doing things together, that I couldn't make the adjustment as you became more distant and unavailable. You had your work to keep you, and all I had was time. So I took up dance, as an instructor, hoping it would temporarily satisfy my craving for us.

He was only supposed to be my dance partner for the competition. That's all! I swear to God, that's all I intended for it to be. Then it all became so confusing. He was always there and you were not. Even when you were home, your dreams had become so attractive and demanding that you failed to respond to my cries for help. I needed you badly. You'd always tell me, "Baby, I'm working on something big!" Do you remember?

What I remember are the vows you and I agreed to. *Do you remember?* "I will be yours in times of plenty and in times of want, in times of sickness and in times of health, in times of joy and in times of sorrow, in times of failure and in times of triumph. I promise to cherish and respect you, to care for and protect you, to comfort and encourage you, and stay with you, for all eternity." You invited another man, a white man, into our marriage, our sacred commitment, and gave him the only thing that matters to me.

Your love has been my paradise, my bridge to God, and without it, I remain trapped in this despicable place. How could you be so low down?

I've never had a desire to put my hands on you inappropriately, but today you've given me a reason to be less than the man I am. I fight every day to hold on to the little dignity that I have left, and now I realize that my love and commitment to you, my reason for choosing death in your honor, is based on a complete and total lie. You have betrayed me in the worst possible way!

I'm dying. Clyde! I said . . . I'mmmm dying.

Dying from what?

Pancreatic cancer. My doctor told me that I have less than six months to live. I found out two weeks ago.

Clyde sat silently, looking down at the floor. He was devastated. Suicidal thoughts attempted to take residence in his mind. Then he thought of Jackson and the eleven young men that he'd strategically guided through and out of the prison system. Each of them turned their lives around and left prison with a plan to serve society. They wrote letters to Clyde regularly to share their triumphs, but never set foot in Reidsville again, as he'd requested. Clyde dismissed the thought of suicide and began to crave the taste of freedom. He lifted his head and looked combatively into Bernadette's eyes.

Tell me something Bernadette! Would you have told me about the affair if you hadn't been diagnosed with a terminal illness?

I've tried to tell you many times, but didn't have the courage. I've suffered a great consequence and paid an enormous debt for my misguided decision.   Waking up without you, taking on this overwhelming shame and guilt, has transformed me in ways you couldn't even imagine. I get drunk daily to help me forget. Cocaine is always in reach whenever I need a fix. The only thing in my life that has been good, *which has kept me alive*, is my Saturday visits with you. I accept responsibility for my role. I was wrong. I need peace, Clyde. Can you please try to understand? For twenty-nine years, I've asked God to forgive me. What I really need now is to know that you forgive me. Please Clyde, will you forgive me?

Get me out of here, Bernadette.

Clyde stood up and walked toward the guard. Though it had only been thirty minutes, the visit was over. Bernadette sat there and cried for nearly an hour. When Clyde returned to his cell, he let out an agonizing scream. He was deeply disturbed and, though his emotions told him to hate Bernadette, his commitment to love, honor, cherish, and respect her took precedence.

To ease his mind and restrain his emotions, Clyde spent a considerable amount of time in prayer during the seventy-two hours which followed. He studied the life of biblical character Joseph, carefully examining the lessons Joseph had to learn before gaining his freedom.

Clyde began to parallel the recession, which began in December 2007, to the famine of Joseph's time. Clyde was delighted to know that he'd adequately prepared Jackson to deliver an economic breakthrough with My Money Works For Me. Then he contemplated what was next for him. "Freedom!" he declared.

On Monday, August 31, 2009, Bernadette contacted and retained Bradford Dale Tillman, an attorney she'd selected from the yellow pages. He seemed to be the right man for the job - at least during the consultation. However, Bernadette knew within a week's time that Clyde didn't have a chance at freedom with Bradford serving as his attorney. Bradford ran into roadblocks at every turn, trying to get the case re-opened. Bernadette paid what she owed and informed Bradford that his services were no longer required.

During her final visit to Reidsville, Bernadette informed Clyde about the trouble Bradford had experienced. Clyde remained hopeful that he'd be free again and told Bernadette that he'd make a call to get some help. Jackson was happy to hear from Clyde, excited about exoneration.

Jackson didn't waste any time. He contacted Julianne Blacksmith-Jones and she told him to go online to **www.InnocenceProject.org** – *a national litigation and public policy organization dedicated to exonerating wrongfully convicted people, through DNA testing.*

Jackson spent a few hours reviewing the information on the website and then contacted Julianne again. She had already phoned in a favor to a Detective James Kendrick, who recommended Stacy Isles-Harrison, a widely respected and successful attorney who specialized in exonerating the wrongfully accused. Stacy booked an appointment to meet with Jackson, Detective James Kendrick, and Bernadette, for Tuesday at 9:00am. Jackson phoned Mrs. Richardson and gave her the appointment information. She thanked him for helping Clyde and said she'd see him on Tuesday morning.

Stacy Isles-Harrison

Chapter 42

Feelings Can Be Deceiving

Be Careful Who You Confide In

Mrs. Richardson arrived thirty minutes early to meet with Stacy and cover the plan of action for presenting her story. She agreed to videotape her deposition and answer questions. Stacy encouraged Mrs. Richardson to provide as much detail as she felt comfortable sharing, particularly information about her relationship with Officer Shawn Reese.

I met Shawn Reese at the dance studio, where I was an instructor. He was an exceptional dancer, a quick learner, and quite charming. After class, he'd stay for extra pointers, and eventually we became dance partners, even friends.

Training for the dance competition allowed Shawn and me to spend many hours together. For three and a half months, we trained non-stop almost every day. Our first-place victory made it all worth it. Though I felt a great sense of accomplishment, what I really wanted to do was to spend time with my husband. Clyde had planned to attend, but decided at the last minute to spend the day working on his big project.

When Shawn and I finished our routine, we returned to our table. I tried to hide my feelings about Clyde's absence, but Shawn knew I was disappointed and felt obligated to cheer me up. When he suggested we go out for drinks, I said, "No, thank you." Then he suggested dinner, and I was all smiles. It was a pleasant atmosphere colored by soft music and romantic lighting. The food, though not outstanding, was acceptable.

Instead of going home after dinner, Shawn and I took a walk through the park. It was just before sunset on February 14, 1980. Being

Valentine's Day, we discussed love and relationships. Shawn spoke of the comfort and satisfaction you experience when someone truly loves you. I listened with an unexpected fascination.

Then my face drew closer to his; my lips prepared for the inevitable. I paused long enough to say, "I should go," and then he kissed me. If only I had known the things to come during the four months which followed.

The attraction between us intensified rapidly. Our dance sessions, now more provocative than ever, set the stage for our afternoon love affair. When the last drop of reason exited my mind, I was left emotionally on fire, eager to explore this strange new world – his world – *dangerous, intoxicating, and mesmerizing.* He took me places sexually that I'd never known with Clyde - places I wish I had never visited.

Shawn showed me kindness and consideration which I absolutely craved. He was tender, thoughtful, and attentive, frequently spending time with me and putting my needs first - *exactly the way Clyde used to care for me.*

Shawn's willingness to explore my world and fill my emptiness made it nearly impossible for me to stop. I somehow tricked myself into believing that Shawn was Clyde. When I looked at Shawn, I imagined Clyde's face, heard Clyde's voice, and felt Clyde's touch. I know it sounds crazy, but that's how I coped. That's how I justified my actions and quieted my conscience.

Then it became so complicated. I was no longer in control and began to see how Shawn had manipulated me through my pain. Still, I was unable to resist; I just couldn't get away from him.

Three weeks into the affair, Shawn showed up at the restaurant while Clyde and I were having dinner. When I saw him, I panicked. Shawn approached our table and introduced himself to Clyde. Their conversation was brief and casual. He shared how much he appreciated me as a dance instructor and offered to pick up our dinner tab. Clyde respectfully declined his offer; they shook hands and Shawn went to his table.

When his date arrived, anger began to consume me, almost to the point that I wanted to confront her. She was much prettier than I and a better dancer. Toni Larson was Shawn's ex-girlfriend. According to Shawn, she divorced her husband and planned to marry him. Things didn't work out. They parted, shortly after the previous year's dance competition.

Seeing the two of them laughing and enjoying each other's company caused the emptiness to return. My head began to throb and my stomach turned queasy. I had hoped that spending time with Clyde would fix things, but it hadn't. Not the dancing. Not the lovemaking. Nothing! I finally admitted to myself that I was in love with Shawn.

Clyde noticed the change in my demeanor and said, "Baby, are you okay?" I lied, "Just a little tired, that's all. Would you please excuse me? I'll be right back."

I went to the ladies room. Shawn followed. He penetrated me quickly. I wanted him to stop, but felt powerless. He dominated me, like never before, repeatedly asking, "Who do you belong to?" Without hesitation, each time I answered, "I belong to you, baby." He climaxed! I fell deeper into despair, hating the person I'd become. I sat there for a while, trying to figure out how to end it, but no end was in sight.

Shawn and Toni were leaving the restaurant as I returned to my seat. He looked back at me and smiled. I asked Clyde if we could finish our meals at home. He said, "Sure, baby."

Clyde did his best to comfort me, to show his undying love for me; it wasn't enough. I'd gone too far, experienced too much of Shawn's forbidden fruit, to be content with Clyde's lovemaking.

I spent most of the weekend in bed, pretending to be sick. That Monday, I phoned the dance studio and canceled my classes for the week. I needed to get Shawn out of my system; I had to avoid him long enough to figure out what to do. After thinking about what I wanted, I decided to give up dance in order to rebuild my relationship with my husband. He needed my support and I needed his love.

I went by the dance studio to pick up my final check, and Shawn was waiting for me when I exited the building. He persuaded me to go for a ride, just to talk, and we ended up at his place.

Shawn started the bath water as soon as we arrived. I placed my things in the chair and turned on some music. He'd set the table and prepared the room for candlelight. He prepared my favorite meal – *baked ziti and French bread* – and placed it in the oven. Shawn lifted the dress above my head, removed my bra and panties and then carried me to my bubble bath oasis. Afterwards, he rubbed lotion on my entire body and massaged my back and shoulders.

We had dinner. It was heaven. I stood. He took my hand. We danced slowly. Our eyes met. He kissed me. I felt him rise. The robe slid down my back. I wanted him. My juices were flowing. I turned. He caressed my back, down to my feet, then up again. I bent over slightly. He tasted me. I turned again. Our tongues made love. He held my face. His eyes disturbed me. The passion had departed. He said, "I love you." I didn't respond. He repeated the words. I stared into his eyes. I felt his pain. He felt mine too. Then he whispered, "I will take care of Clyde."

Immediately, I came to my senses, snapped out of the spell, pushed away from him and said, "What did you say?" He laughed. "You think it's funny?" I asked. "You belong to me now," he countered.

I declared to him as well as to myself, "I love my husband. You are a mistake. A big mistake! I'm leaving now." I got dressed and headed toward the door. Surprisingly, he didn't try to convince me to stay. Shawn turned on our favorite song, reached for my hand and asked, "Can I have one last dance before you walk out of my life?"

I said, "No!" He became violent. Shawn pinned my face against the door, with his forearm across my back. I could feel my face swelling, my eye blackening. I thought, "How will I explain this to Clyde?"

Then Shawn brought me back to the present. He jammed his hand between my legs and pressed up firmly. Then he asked, "Who does this belong to?" Terrified, I responded, "It belongs to you, baby!"

I tried to calm him, but it only made him press harder. His fingers penetrated me. He forced me to my knees and placed his erection on my mouth, his hand gripping my head. I took him in and worked him over until he closed his eyes and gave up his power. I squeezed and twisted his male anatomy until that bastard hit the floor. Then I knocked him in the head with my shoe.

I moved quickly, grabbing my purse and his keys. He ran out after me, holding the eye that I had blackened. I put the car in drive and floored it. The police station was a few miles away. I decided against it. My secret had to remain. Clyde could never find out. I was done with Shawn Reese.

For two months, I didn't see Shawn. Upon returning from the grocery store, I opened the door and there he sat watching <u>Days of Our Lives</u>. Shawn walked over, kissed me gently on the cheek, and went out the front door.

How did he get into your house?

I don't know. I checked the doors and windows. Everything was locked, so I figured he'd made a duplicate key. I contacted a locksmith and had the locks replaced.

Was there any contact between you and Reese during the two month period?

No calls. That was one of our rules. We never spoke on the phone or dined in public. However, before the affair began, we frequently had lunch together at the diner across from the dance studio. Sometimes other students would join us. Other times we were alone.

Are you suggesting that others from the dance studio knew about your affair with Reese?

No, we were careful or, at least, intended to be discreet.

I see. What happened next?

Shawn started showing up everywhere I went. I wanted to tell Clyde, but I couldn't. Sometimes Shawn would just follow me around in his police cruiser. Finally, I confronted him and he stopped for about two weeks. The next time I saw Shawn, he was pulling into my driveway.

He knocked on the door and said, "Hello, darling, I've missed you terribly. Can we talk?" I said, "There's nothing to talk about. Would you please leave? My husband is on his way home for lunch." It was a lie, but I thought it might get him to leave. He said, "Sweetheart, please open the door." Foolishly, I did, and the nightmare continued.

Shawn removed his gun from the holster, pointed it in my direction, and forced his way into the house. I backed up slowly, terrified, recalling how he'd hurt me before. He walked toward me, placed his hands on my face, close to my neck, and then ran his finger across my throat. I gasped before daringly telling him, "Leave, or I'll call the police." Shawn said, "I am the police!" and placed his gun firmly against my cheek. He switched off the safety and placed the barrel in my mouth.

As if that were not enough to scare the living daylights out of me, he muttered, "This gun and badge give me the power to do whatever the hell I want, and today I'm going to make you pay. Then we can say it's over, bitch."

Shawn let go of my throat and placed the gun on the end table. He began removing his clothes - first his belt, and then his shirt and pants. As he pulled the pant leg over his ankle, I bolted for the phone, and he struck me with his forearm. Before I could get up, Shawn was on top of me. Blood poured from my nose. I screamed and begged him to stop, but knew he wasn't going to when I saw the madness in his eyes.

So I dug my nails into his face. He twisted my wrists, flipped me over, and pinned my arms behind my back. Then he began ripping away my clothes. Before he could get my panties off, another car pulled up into the driveway. It was my husband.

> *Hold up!* I thought you said that you lied about your husband coming home for lunch. This seems a bit coincidental.

I thought it was odd too, because Clyde never came home in the middle of the day. When he left for work in the morning, I usually didn't see him again until after 7:00pm. I found out years later from Clyde that a neighbor had contacted him.

So there was a witness at the scene of the crime?

I guess you could say a potential witness.

Do you know who might have made that call to Mr. Richardson?

As far as names, it couldn't have been Paulette because she would have told me. Paulette was the neighborhood watchdog; she knew everybody's comings and goings. Maybe it was Karen Goldman or Traci Morrison. Their shift at the hospital started at 3:00pm, so they were usually home during this time.

Okay. Someone called your husband and he rushed home. Did he attempt to call you first?

Actually, come to think about it, the phone did ring. Twice, someone tried to call, but of course I couldn't answer. Reese had me pinned on the floor.

Then what happened?

When Clyde opened the front door, he rushed to my rescue. But Shawn was much stronger and faster than Clyde. They struggled for a minute and then Shawn hit Clyde with a vase. Clyde fell to the floor. When I realized Shawn was heading for his gun, I beat him to it and said, "If you don't stop, I'll shoot you." He responded, "Give me what I came here for," and lunged at me. That's when I shot him!

You shot him? Whoa! Now that's interesting. Tell me, who called the cops and did they show up right away?

I don't know who called them. The last thing I remember was the gunshot and Clyde saying, "I'll fix this, sweetheart." When I came to at the hospital, the police were waiting to get a statement. The officer told me my husband was in custody for murder. I told them about the attempted rape, but said nothing of the affair.

Why did you withhold information?

Fear and guilt, I suppose. Plus, I really didn't know what to do, especially about the affair. I'd always consulted with Clyde before making major decisions. I figured we might have a chance to win a self-defense case with the right attorney.

However, when I finally talked to Clyde, he informed me that he'd accepted a plea for a lesser charge. He made me promise never to say anything to anyone about the incident with the officer. He's never told me why. I said, "But, Clyde, we didn't do anything wrong. He tried to rape me." Clyde responded, "I know, baby. It's best this way. It's for your protection. *Trust me!* I love you, Bernadette."

Does Mr. Richardson know about your affair?
Yes, he knows. I told him a little over a week ago. He was angry, but hopeful that he might be exonerated. Clyde deserves to be free, and I trust that you will do what is necessary to make this happen?

When Stacy noticed that Mrs. Richardson was trembling, she said, "That's enough for today." She walked Mrs. Richardson to her car and said, "Are you okay? Do I need to have someone drive you home?" Mrs. Richardson replied, "No, but thank you for offering." Stacy responded, "Okay, I will be in contact with you in a few days. There's a lot of work to be done."

Mrs. Richardson, still shaken up, said, "I don't have much time. I'm dying of pancreatic cancer and want to see Clyde free before I close my eyes for the last time." "I assure you, we'll do everything we can," said Stacy.

Chapter 43

Guilty or Not Guilty

The Search For Evidence Begins

Stacy met with Detective Kendrick and his investigative team the following morning – Gina Ruffin *(Researcher/Journalist)*, Max Hager *(Medical Examiner/Investigator)*, and Lindsay Baynes *(Computer and Technology Expert)*. Jackson Gray and Stacy's paralegal, Christina Flannigan, also attended the meeting.

Stacy had spent a significant portion of the previous day with Zack Dawson – *a trial consultant* – studying the video recording of Mrs. Richardson's deposition. She and Zack put together a timeline of events to help the team determine which gaps needed to be filled. Stacy replayed the video deposition for Gina, Max, and Lindsay.

Team, after carefully reviewing Mrs. Richardson deposition, here's what we need to find out:

Who phoned Mr. Richardson at his job and what did they tell him? Jackson, get in contact with Mr. Richardson today and get me an answer. I'd like to hear his side of the story, particularly the details of his plea bargain.

We can wrap this up in as little as six weeks if we build a strong case, backed by solid evidence. I do not want to go to trial, unless it's absolutely necessary. Our client's future should be determined by careful presentation of the facts, rather than by a jury of his peers. We must provide new information that will undoubtedly change the outcome of the case.

District Attorney Sax will not take a case to court unless she can win. Sax has an impressive track record of cases defending women who have been domestically abused, so it's in our best interest to prove that Officer Shawn Reese had a pattern of violent behavior against women. We will aggressively exploit and penetrate this point of interest, since it is her soft spot.

We also need to develop a trial strategy, aimed at persuading a jury to view Reese not as a cop, but as an unbalanced, disturbed, and unsettled individual. This will serve as our "Plan B" if, and only if, a trial is required.

Gina, find out if Reese was married. If nothing turns up, locate and contact his ex-girlfriends, beginning with Toni Larson. Mrs. Richardson said he was a charmer, so it's probable that Reese kept a company of women – *women who may have experienced his violent outbursts.* We need to find them and prove Reese was out of control, a maniac, to be precise.

Finally, Mrs. Richardson said she pulled the trigger. What does the Chief Medical Examiner's (CME) report indicate about Reese's cause of death? Mrs. Richardson indicated that Reese struck her with enough force to knock her to the floor and cause her nose to bleed profusely. Was her blood found on his hand? Was his face scratched from her nails?

Max, this one's for you. Review the autopsy report to find out what you can about the murder weapon and actual cause of death. At the time of Reese's death, the Chief Medical Examiner was Montgomery

Charles, meticulous and well-trained, one of the best in the country. He was known for writing the most detailed and thorough autopsy reports. If Mrs. Richardson handled the weapon and clawed Reese's face, it will be documented.

Also, check the medical records for Mrs. Richardson's examination. I'm positive there's a rape kit if Mrs. Richardson suffered the sexual assault presented in her deposition. She never mentioned anything about penetration, but Reese was on top of her and may have left seminal fluid on her clothes.

Lindsay, find me something in Reese's personnel file with the Fulton County PD. The Georgia Open Records Act grants us access to this information. Review Fincher vs. State of Georgia (1998) for details on how to legally handle this information. Although Reese is deceased, we must still act within the boundaries established by the justice system. Also, collect material about important cases covered during 1980. I'd like to know what challenges existed for the police department, particularly in Fulton County and the City of Atlanta.

Keep in mind as we put together this case that it is a black-on-white crime against a police officer. The judge and district attorney will eat us alive us if we don't have all our ducks in a row.

Detective Kendrick, I need you to review <u>The Trials of Darryl Hunt</u> on DVD and contact the people involved. They should be able to point out the racially-biased pitfalls to avoid. A list of phone numbers and email addresses is enclosed in your packet to help expedite your data collection. Be sure not to mention pertinent details about this case.

It is critical for everyone to contact Christina as soon as you have the information I've requested. She will forward it to Zack, and he'll update the presentation and timeline. We'll meet again on Friday, same time. By the way, we need to act quickly and discreetly. Let's try to wrap up the data collection within seven days.

Be careful not to draw any attention to this case and focus only on uncovering the facts relevant to helping Mr. Richardson gain his freedom. Leave the inconsequential facts buried. And remember Locard's Exchange Principle: Every contact leaves a trace, so don't come back empty-handed. No matter how much someone tries to clean up a crime scene, something is generally left behind. It may not be easily uncovered, or even be visible to the human eye, but it's almost impossible to take any kind of violent action without leaving some evidence behind.

Chapter 44

More Than Just The Facts

The Proof Is In The Presentation

Lindsay dived right into it. Working twenty-four hours straight on a case wasn't uncommon – a trait she'd picked up from her father, J. Randall Baynes, Director of the Information Technology Division for the FBI. Lindsay talked with her father almost daily, especially when she was working on a big case. Over the years, they've thoroughly enjoyed the process of hunting for the relevant facts, as well as using computers and other technology to solve difficult cases.

Hi daddy. Sorry I've missed your calls for the last few days. How are you?

> Hey, baby girl. Doing just fine. Just excited to know what you're working on.

This is a good one! Deception. Betrayal. Misconduct. Infidelity. And murder. All the elements of a seductively engaging soap opera.

> My kind of story. Go on.

Twenty-nine years ago, an Atlanta man, African American in descent, was convicted of murdering a white Fulton County police officer. The police report indicates that he, the police officer, was responding to a 911 domestic disturbance call.   The wife of the convicted man presented us a totally different story. She claims that an affair she'd ended with the officer three months earlier had brought him to her doorstep. She was doing the guy, frequently, for about six months, and then suddenly has a change of heart? Whatever!

Her husband, supposedly at work on the day of the shooting, arrived just in time to save the day. After fighting with the officer and getting his butt kicked, the gun went off. *Officer dead. Battered woman. No witnesses. Zilch! Nada! Goose egg! Damn!* What a helluva situation to be in. And get this; he didn't even pull the trigger. She shot the officer and then hid the affair from her husband until just a few weeks ago. Bet he was pissed when he learned the truth. Anyway, he settled for a plea bargain and is serving a life sentence with no parole down at Reidsville.

My role in this *just-getting-my-needs-met-poor-excuse-for-a-wife-drama* is to uncover the seemingly dark past of the officer and then exploit the integrity of the police organization to which he belonged. I'm not sure how I'm going to approach this case, but our team is operating under the assumption that the officer had a violent history with women. In the end, we hope to uncover and present a series of facts which will undoubtedly prove the convicted man's innocence and give him back his freedom.

I take it, you believe the wife has withheld pertinent information?
I do. But that's not what's bugging me. Several years have passed since the incident, and I've never worked on a case involving a police organization.

That's not exactly true. Remember the Honeywell case involving the judge?
Oh yeah! The Waffle House waitress in Carolina.

Similar time frame; same investigative process. We begin with what we have. And there are four elements in your story that we can explore, examine, and connect.
Fulton County PD . . .
Atlanta . . .
Black-on-white crime . . .
and 1980.

And the significance of these four things is what?

>Not so fast, dear. Take your time and think it through. Let's start with the police report. Was a 911 tape produced to substantiate the police report's domestic disturbance allegation?

To my knowledge, there's no tape.

>Did the incident take place at a house or an apartment?

A house.

>Is the house still standing and in its original design, meaning no major remodeling?

The house is still standing. In fact, the convicted man's wife still leases the property. I will ask the attorney to contact her about structural changes to the home.

>Good. You may need to stop by and take some pictures of the house. Be sure that your client's wife accompanies you.

Just a second! I'm sending the attorney a message.

>Done?

Yes.

>In 1980, was the crime scene address within Atlanta's city limits?

It's within Atlanta's city limits today.

>You're right, but that's not how we do things. You want to be absolutely certain about everything used to support your case. Research the 1952 Annexation of Atlanta and you'll find your answer.

Okay.

>So far, we uncovered that there's probably not a 911 tape to justify the officer's visit and the crime, more than likely, took place at an address within Atlanta's city limits. What is the link between the crime scene address and the Fulton County PD?

There is no link! *Whoa! Atlanta PD should have been dispatched, not Fulton County.*

Exactly! I taught you well.

Bragging, are we?

Can't help it. You make me proud.

Thanks, Papa J. You know . . . you mentioned earlier that four things came to mind. How do black-on-white crime and 1980 fit into the equation?

You were paying attention. Impressive! The first point, black-on-white crime, more specifically, crime against a police officer, has been the incentive used by some officers and other public authorities to break the laws which they are paid to enforce. Their impatience with and disbelief in the justice system have given way to a mindset designed to rob not only the black, but also the red, yellow, brown, and white citizens of this country. Your client was robbed, even if the evidence will confirm he is guilty. The authorities never tried the case to establish that justice was being served. Instead, they allowed his ignorance of the law to influence a poor decision. Still with me?

I'm still with you.

The second point is more complex. In 1980, the City of Atlanta was on the brink of a race war due to the Atlanta Child Murders. Young black children from poor neighborhoods were disappearing left and right, and then turning up dead. The City of Atlanta was under great pressure to find and prosecute the person or group responsible for the murders.

How do you think this information can help me with my case?

I'm not sure, sweat pea. What I do know is the City of Atlanta and Atlanta PD stood in the world's spotlight. Families across the nation watched the news with a hopeless expectation, praying that the nightmare would come to an end. Politicians and law enforcement agencies continued to make a mockery of the justice system by disregarding the unique characteristics of the case. Rather than conduct a thorough investigation, they concluded that the murders in these poor neighborhoods were consistent with known statistics, so no one should be alarmed.

The black community was outraged and demanded something be done immediately. Then, in 1981, police arrested Wayne Williams, a black man, and pinned the twenty-nine murders on him.

The problem I have with this conviction is that prosecutors didn't provide substantial evidence to prove Williams had committed the crimes. Their careless application of the governing laws caused the American public, particularly members of the black community, to fear that the real perpetrator was still at large. Some think the Klan was behind it all, due to their hatred for the city's black administration. I'm not settled on this one. However, I do suspect that some unhealthy tension was brewing between the black politicians and white business elite.

As far as the Williams case is concerned, a documentary was created titled Echo of Murder. The story unfolds as an investigation being conducted by two journalists of a major magazine. For you, this documentary could very well shed some light on how ill-prepared police organizations, in and around Atlanta, were in their ability to quickly and intelligently respond to and solve a murder case. I have it in my DVD collection if you'd like to stop by the house and pick it up.

Yes, I'd like that. I'll stop by later today. Does the movie discuss whether or not other police agencies joined forces with Atlanta PD to work on this case?

> Yes, but the entire operation was influenced by politicians. A task force was formed, including officers from the counties in which bodies had been recovered. The task force, as I understand, lacked the leadership, competence, organization, and focus needed to make it effective. The police just weren't prepared to handle murder investigations, especially of this nature and magnitude.

What can you tell me about the leadership and reputation of the Fulton County PD during this time period?

> An exceptional organization! Though only five years old at the time, the Fulton County PD was well respected. In fact, they were the first police department in the Atlanta area to receive accreditation from CALEA, which stands for <u>Commission on Accreditation for Law Enforcement Agencies</u>. I believe it was 1987 when they earned their accreditation.

Seven years. I wonder. It might be a strrrrretch. Tell me this, do you think it's likely that a police organization would initiate a cover-up, in order to protect their good standing and stay on track for accreditation through CALEA?

> It's a possibility, but I'm not sure if Police Chief Chafin would have allowed it. Let's think this through. If the murdered police officer was guilty of deliberately neglecting to follow police procedure, it could have certainly compromised the organization's impeccable reputation. Then again, the organization could have unknowingly participated.

> As I said before, some police officers will do whatever is necessary to justify their stories. These secrets are usually taken to the grave,

but sometimes you get lucky and run across an officer with a conscience. I hope this is the case for your client's sake.

Until this person surfaces, we'll work with the evidence left behind by the murdered police officer. Remember Locard's Exchange Principle – *every contact leaves a trace.* I'm certain that his documented reputation as an officer holds the key to unlock clues which will lead us to other relevant facts. What was his name?

Shawn Reese.

Great! I will make a phone call to see what kind of reputation Reese had during his time with the Fulton County PD. I should have something for you by tomorrow. Can you think of anything else that we need to discuss before I go?

No. I have enough information to work with until we speak again.

Excellent. I'm going to take the rest of my sandwich back to the office because I have 2:00pm Director's meeting. It's been fun and maybe I'll see you tonight.

OK. Love you, Daddy, and thanks for lunch!

Love you too, sweet pea.

The following morning, Lindsay received a text message from her father. Call me as soon as you can. She phoned right away.

Morning, Daddy! What did you find out?

There was an Internal Affairs investigation. Contact the GBI Open Records Unit at 404-270-8527. Also, he had a partner. That's all I can tell you.

Thanks, Daddy. You're the best! I'll call right now. Love you.

Love you too, sweet pea. Talk to you soon.

Lindsay requested and received a copy of the Internal Affairs investigation against Reese. She contacted Christina. She also phoned Stacy about three alleged victims referenced in the report. Stacy passed the information on to Gina and Detective Kendrick. He made a few calls to find out about Reese's ex-partner.

Jackson met with Mr. Richardson and learned about a package Mrs. Richardson hadn't disclosed during the video deposition. In the summer of 2008, Mrs. Richardson ran into Paulette Simpson – her ex-neighbor – while shopping at the Arbor Place Mall in Douglasville. The two of them hadn't seen each other for almost fifteen years and decided to meet for coffee after they'd finished shopping.

They talked about what happened the day of the shooting. Paulette apologized several times before telling Mrs. Richardson about a package she'd kept hidden for twenty-eight years.

Paulette was home when Shawn Reese pulled into Bernadette's driveway. She witnessed the whole affair and contacted Clyde at his job. She also phoned the police when she heard the two men struggling. Atlanta PD officers were at the crime scene minutes after the fatal gunshot.

Paulette, a freelance photographer and journalism major, documented her stories with pictures. She'd photographed Reese on several occasions watching Bernadette's home from his police cruiser. Some photos captured Reese snooping around the house.

After the shooting, Paulette planned to tell Bernadette, but was persuaded by her husband to stay out of it. He was concerned for the safety of their two boys. Paulette reluctantly agreed, but decided to preserve the evidence until the time was right to reveal it.

When Mr. Richardson learned of the package, he was hopeful, knowing its contents increased his likelihood for exoneration. Yet, he was troubled by the thought of losing Bernadette. In spite of her mistake, her love still made his heart tingle.

Jackson captured the details of the plea bargain in his phone. When he returned to his vehicle, Jackson contacted Christina to pass on the information. He then phoned Stacy to schedule a one-on-one to discuss Mr. Richardson's concerns about his case and the contents of the package. During the meeting, Stacy agreed to keep the package confidential until enough evidence had been collected by the investigative team to build a rock solid case. Stacy's eyes filled with fury as she listened to the details of Mr. Richardson's plea bargain. She contacted Christina and asked her to locate the public defender who handled Mr. Richardson's case.

When Max checked the autopsy report, it specified that prints had been lifted from the alleged murder weapon. Mrs. Richardson was a match; Mr. Richardson was not.

Detective Kendrick phoned Lindsay and asked her to find out what she could about Officer John Kincaid. It didn't take her long. Kincaid was no longer a police officer, but a restaurant owner. He decided to end his career in law enforcement shortly after Reese's funeral. Lindsay contacted the restaurant to find out when Kincaid would be available.

Max made another promising discovery while comparing the chief examiner's report to Mrs. Richardson's hospital examination. Shawn Reese had seminal fluid on his boxers; the same seminal fluid found on Mrs. Richardson's panties. Skin removed from her nails was also a match for Reese. Max concluded that the attempted rape probably occurred and phoned Christina with the update.

Detective Kendrick met with Kincaid, who shared that he'd covered for Reese in more than a dozen acts of misconduct against women, most initiated during a traffic stop. Kincaid said, "Reese had this thing for married women – women with something to lose. They found his charm irresistible. When they'd try to leave him, they'd meet the monster. It's like he was on this mission to punish women who cheated. The fatality in the Richardson case made me rethink the whole loyalty thing. I wanted to say something, but knew it wasn't wise to come right out and tell my story. Over the years, I've sent Mr. Richardson several books about law, hoping he'd try for an appeal. But he never did. He deserves to be free."

Stacy arrived at the dance studio and interviewed two women who'd been Mrs. Richardson's students. She also interviewed Toni Larson, the dancer Reese showed up with at the restaurant. To Stacy's surprise, Toni not only knew about Reese's obsession with Mrs. Richardson, but had also been working undercover with Internal Affairs. Stacy sensed that Toni had developed more than a professional connection to Reese. Her hunch was confirmed when Toni admitted their plans to get married. Toni resigned shortly after Shawn's death.

The next morning, Stacy and Detective Kendrick met with Zack to view an early version of the presentation. Detective Kendrick's conversation with Kincaid revealed that he and Shawn Reese were off duty the day of the shooting.

During the two weeks that followed, the investigative team worked around the clock to arrange the facts, fill in the gaps, and build a case they expectantly hoped would exonerate Mr. Richardson.

Thanks to a friend, Stacy received a phone call from Peter Yack, the public defender assigned to Mr. Richardson's original case. Peter was no longer an attorney, but a journalist and author of true crime novels, involving corrupt individuals in the fields of law and justice. His deposition provided information to help Stacy's team close the gap between Mr. Richardson's arrest and his acceptance of the plea bargain. With Mr. Richardson's permission, Peter explained to Stacy that refusing the plea bargain would have meant a potential life sentence for Bernadette *and* Clyde. This confirmed what she'd learned from Jackson about the plea.

Though Peter recommended taking it to trial, Mr. Richardson declined because he felt it was too risky. In the end, Mr. Richardson's fear and incompetence in the area of law caused him great pain. However, he did study the law books sent by Kincaid. His confidence now rested in the justice system he knew could prove his innocence.

The presentation created by Zack provided more than enough evidence to convince the judge and district attorney of police misconduct. Paulette's twelve incriminating photographs of Shawn Reese, the autopsy report, phone records, plea bargain details, Internal Affairs investigation, and depositions from Toni Larson, Peter Yack, and three victims of Reese's traffic-stop initiated love triangles sealed the deal. John Kincaid requested to remain anonymous, yet provided enough evidence to confirm what Stacy had speculated about Reese's behavior toward women, as well as his obsession with Mrs. Richardson.

Stacy prepared and filed the extraordinary motion for new trial on the grounds of evidence fabrication, coerced confession, suppression of exculpatory evidence, and knowing use of false testimony. A hearing was quickly granted by the Court.

Clyde Richardson

Chapter 45

The Eyes of Justice

Twenty-Nine Years Later

Though overwhelmed with excitement, Jackson stood nonchalantly by the black cherry 2010 Cadillac CTS he'd purchased for Mr. Richardson as a coming home gift.   This work of art exhibited elegance and power, distinction and personality, exquisiteness and prestige.

The cashmere interior, complemented by a delicate cocoa underscore, impressive wood trim, chrome accents, and a metallic finish, gave birth to an atmosphere fit only for a distinguished gentleman.

Decorative French-stitched seams exuded style and sophistication, allowing the cashmere leather to yield unparalleled comfort and stunning workmanship.   The sweeping chrome-dipped instrument panel maximized interior space, parading motorcycle-inspired gauges to signify high performance, instant gratification, and breathtaking enjoyment.

Visually, it illustrated the likes of Michelangelo, Botticelli, Van Gogh, Bruegel, and Tansey.   Sensually, it initiated the fascination and appeal most of us experience while witnessing a human body in the perfect form.   Lean muscle and sophisticated curves fused with character, charisma, and captivating looks.

The three-point six liter Direct Injection V6 engine boasted three hundred and four horsepower.   Let the salesperson tell it, and he'd convince you this car was almost *powerful and fast enough* to take a stock GT Mustang in the quarter mile.   Its high fuel efficiency, coupled with a system optimized to run on regular unleaded gasoline, unequivocally made this Cadillac the choice luxury performance sedan.

Top off these remarkable features with a fully integrated navigation system, making it next to impossible for you to get lost, concert-quality Bose sound for days when you simply want to cruise and be serenaded, heated and cooled powered seats, leg room sufficient for a ball player, nineteen-inch polished wheels that sparkle while you're waiting for the traffic light to change, and fully independent suspension for superior handling.

This Cadillac CTS combined unrivaled sportiness with sublime comfort, never compromising either for a moment. Its desire to be driven . . . *undeniable!*

As the gate opened, Mr. Richardson stood erect, a man ready to explore this new world and live life to the fullest. His eyes expressed a deep appreciation for the opportunity to once again *choose his preferences and define his boundaries.* His next few actions were intriguing, so I waited by the car and carefully observed.

He stepped through the gate and paused, looked up, lifted his hands as if preparing to catch something from the sky, closed his eyes, smiled, and then bowed his head. I continued to study him, silently. Mr. Richardson appeared to be receiving something valuable, instructions perhaps, because he nodded his head several times, as if to say yes. This went on for about ten minutes. He recovered, thanked God, and then looked in my direction.

I met him half way with open arms, and we embraced. This pivotal moment redefined what freedom meant to both of us. It prompted me to consider that every minute of every day was incomparable, unique, and the opportunity to create or destroy. I've chosen to create; *first in my mind,* then with my words, and finally through experienced and sagacious hands. Mr. Richardson has served me well, as counselor and confidant.

Our embrace, though dramatic and joyful, was without sound. We savored the moment, father and son, meeting for what seemed like the very first time. It felt as though he'd gone on a trip to a faraway place and was finally coming home to stay. I recounted the series of events which had led to this moment and acknowledged the people who believed in him enough to pave his path to freedom.

I handed him the keys and pointed in the car's direction. He turned his head slowly. His smile widened as he inquired, "For me?" I nodded in agreement. He walked around the vehicle unhurriedly, taking in every detail. He touched it gently, the way a skilled man massages a woman before making love to her.

It was truly a sight to see – a man giving honor not to things, *but to privilege.* Though he craved this material possession, his affection for the gift was offered first to God.

As he rounded the corner to take in the chrome along the bumper, sculpted body lines surrounding the rear window and lights, as well as the signature Cadillac emblem arranged at the center of the trunk, just above the chrome trimming, I reflected upon the conversations we'd had about cars. When we weren't discussing law or economics, it was cars. The colors, styles, engines, performance, embellishments, and what it would be like to have a garage full of our favorite automobiles.

His father was a caddy man and so was my grandfather. For me, it was the Fastback Mustang, *supercharged and undeniably attractive.* Geovana has learned over the years, though my love for her is unrivaled, that my car, Chynadoll is a touchy feely kind of girl and requires many hours alone with me every Saturday afternoon. Men and women alike tell me how beautiful she is after a fresh wash and wax.

Initially, I was going to drive Chynadoll to pick up Mr. Richardson. Then Geovana persuaded me to do something special for him. She and I had a blast dressing up in our finest threads and going to various Cadillac dealerships for the sales pitch and test drive. Afterwards, we'd have dinner and return to a quiet home to make love for the rest of the evening. We'd drop our children off at their grandmother's house, and she'd take them to school the following day.

This was a special time for us to reconnect and redefine our relationship. Prior to this, intimacy had taken on a new form, one which I didn't quite understand, but went along with because of my love for Geovana. Sex had almost become a thing of the past – once or twice a month for nearly two years. Though our sexual experiences remained amazing, I wanted to experience Geovana more often.

Also, I deeply craved the desire to make a child from my own seed. Don't get me wrong. I'd give my life for Alicia and Alexander. They are my children.

However, when I am vulnerable, the pain finds a way to creep in and remind me of the circumstances which brought them into this world. Intense anger transforms into deep pain, and then I'd find myself in a dark place feeling powerless and defeated.   It takes everything in me to break free and reach for her love, which has never diminished.

I just wanted wanted Geovana to be there, with me, completely. Little did I know, she'd never left my side. I'd allowed my desire to cloud my perception, forgetting totally about the superior quality of her love. It was a challenge we needed to work through together.

My brother, Psoloman, told me he'd experienced a similar challenge before he and Antoinette conceived their third child earlier this year. He said, "Hang in there, bro. She needs time and love. The kind of love which sustained you during the nine years the two of you were apart." Though it helped a little, it did not give me what I wanted – a child conceived between Geovana and me.

Eventually, I built up the courage to share my dilemma with Mr. Richardson. He provided the stability and focus I needed to love her, as well as myself, through this pain. His counsel was always the same, "Love endures long and is patient and kind."

Back then, I understood the endurance piece, but struggled with being patient *and* kind; that is, affectionate, gentle, and restorative, for as long as was necessary to inspire the desired change. Over time, I discovered it was about me. I need to upgrade my skills. I had to learn how to cultivate family and expand my influence.

Mr. Richardson taught me the word *husband* means to cultivate, farm, direct, prepare, enrich, promote, and refine. I had to lead the way, trusting that Geovana would follow and support me. In time, after I'd fostered attractive leadership skills, it paid off and blessed our family.

During the early stages of my leadership development, I'd take a drive to prevent unkind words from multiplying the hurt Geovana had already experienced. I'd tell her I needed to clear my mind of some ugly thoughts. I also told her that I'd return home in a few hours.

She informed me later she would have preferred me to hold her, but appreciated me letting her know I was coming back. This made it easier for her to support my coping mechanism and assist in my growth. After the drive, I'd stop by the gym, burnout on weights, and shower.

When I returned home a few hours later, Geovana always had something delicious waiting for me at the dinner table. We'd eat together and then enjoy a Lifetime movie or two, cuddled up on the couch under a blanket.

Mr. Richardson monitored my progress. Once my habits began to change, he challenged me stay and face my Goliath, for it was the only way I'd develop the skills to fight back and win. He communicated ideas about restoration and patience. He encouraged me to use love as a healing tool. He demonstrated how to seek God for wisdom, or what he called the next right action.

I spent a considerable amount of time studying James chapter one. Geovana often joined me. We expressed our concerns, examined our motives, and expanded our love.

Then I felt a tapping on my shoulder. Mr. Richardson had been watching me travel down memory lane. He said, "It must have been a good experience. You were smiling the whole time. Are you ready to go?" I said, "Yes. Let's get out of here. Would you like me to drive?" He quickly responded, "Oh, no! I've been waiting a long time for this experience. I'll drive a few miles and then let you take us home. Geovana sent me a driver's manual a few weeks ago. Let's plan a visit to the DMV for first thing Monday."

We got into the car and Mr. Richardson said, "Thank you for this fine automobile, Jackson. Now tell me, how is your relationship with Geovana?" I responded, "Exciting! Shopping for your dream car during the past few months has allowed me to realize a dream of my own. Geovana informed me this morning that she's pregnant."

He smiled and said, "That's wonderful. I'd do anything for a chance to raise a family with Bernadette. I'm not sure how to handle this situation, this pain I feel for being robbed of fatherhood."

I looked at him and responded, "No, Dad! That's not true. You've been a father to many. No doubt about it. You've raised a nation of twelve, sort of like Jacob, except we love and build upon each other. No envy. No jealousy. No strife. Just love, skill, and passion. I read the Charles Swindoll book on Joseph that you asked me to purchase. Your copy is in your room at our house. Maybe we can discuss it, once you've had an opportunity to digest the material. I believe it certainly applies to the life you've lived, as well as the challenges you may be facing as you begin to rebuild your life. Whatever the case, I've got your back."

He started the engine and we drove away from that disgraceful place. The conversation was light during the four-hour trip back to Atlanta, but the music played non-stop. I'd copied all his favorites to the hard drive - *The Spinners, The O'Jays, The Temptations, Marvin Gaye, Roberta Flack, Donny Hathaway, Harold Melvin and The Bluenotes, Sam Cooke, and Tina Turner.* I knew most of the songs, so we sang them together for the duration of the trip.

When we turned onto my street, cars lined the curb and filled the driveway. It was the day after Thanksgiving, and we'd already decided to postpone our celebration until Mr. Richardson was home.

Alicia and Alexander were the first to meet and greet Mr. Richardson, followed by Geovana. Next were Stacy, Max, Gina, Lindsay, and Detective Kendrick. When he went inside, to his surprise, was his wife, Bernadette. Though her health was quickly declining, she managed the strength to be there for his celebration and return.

The Life$TYLE Harmony team was also present to celebrate Mr. Richardson's freedom release party: Psoloman and Antoinette, Dr. Yuma and Kaiya, Tai Lynn and Kado, as well as Professor Marcelle and his wife Elaine. Mr. Richardson blessed the meal, thanking God for love, family, forgiveness, and the opportunity to begin again.

After dinner, I drove Mr. Richardson and Bernadette back to the hospital where he stayed until her final breath. He told me they got to know each other again in ten short days. They spoke nothing of the affair during those precious moments, only the love.

In the six months that followed, Mr. Richardson spent many hours studying the Bible and conversing with God. During this time, he met someone who extended him her friendship and support. When he emerged, you could see the contentment in his eyes and vitality in his step. God had restored him, renovated and equipped him for something new.

He met her at the coffee shop. Not a Starbucks, but just as satisfying. Actually, they'd met before, but this time he noticed something different about her smile. The feeling was mutual and their friendship evolved.

Her complexion was stunning – coffee-colored skin, soft cheek bones and full lips, with a radiant smile. Charlena, a widow, hadn't been with a man since the death of her husband. Mr. Richardson spoke of her daily, and the two of them began a courtship like none I've ever witnessed.

Unlike young love, reckless and wild, their love represented a degree of maturity which only God could engineer. It was based on true friendship, an essential ingredient missing from most relationships today. When the time was right, Mr. Richardson asked Geovana and me if he could invite Charlena to dinner. We agreed.

He was somewhat embarrassed when he learned that we already knew he was in love with my mother. Whenever she came around, his infectious smile gave it away. The kids were excited. Alexander kept laughing and acting silly. Alicia kept grinning while covering her face. Finally, Mr. Richardson said to Alexander, "Boy, what's wrong with you?" We all burst out laughing. This was the first of many wonderful meals together. It was during these meals that we learned the importance of family.

As their relationship evolved, he and Mom began attending services at 12Stone Church in Lawrenceville, and he got a place of his own. Watching the two of them gave Geovana and me a sneak preview of our future as a couple.

The manner in which Mr. Richardson expressed his love to my mother was exciting and attractive. They have monthly love competitions to promote a deeper and life-inspiring love. Neither will allow their love to be outdone.

Their love is so powerful that I've often shared with Geovana that they could probably make a baby just looking into each other's eyes. I've evolved because of them; Geovana and I are inseparable physically, emotionally, and spiritually because of the lessons they've taught us. God has blessed our union.

During my imprisonment, Mr. Richardson taught me with books and words. In our freedom, he has taught me through the quality of his life and the preeminence of his love for my mother. I strive daily to reproduce their kind of love in my marriage to Geovana, and I hope one day to be able to share Mr. Richardson's *love formula* with the world through the Life$TYLE Harmony Game. In the end, which is really the beginning, families will be families again.

Two people are better off than one, for they can help each other succeed. If one person falls, the other can reach out and help. But someone who falls alone is in real trouble. Likewise, two people lying close together can keep each other warm. But how can one be warm alone? A person standing alone can be attacked and defeated, but two can stand back-to-back and conquer. Three are even better, for a triple-braided cord is not easily broken. Ecclesiastes 4:9-12 (NLT)

Mr. Richardson said these words to my mother, before going down on one knee, taking her left hand, and making it sparkle. He looked into her eyes, as the congregation silently observed. A teardrop rounded her cheek, moistening the side of her mouth, before falling to its destination. He felt her love upon his hand seconds before asking her to stay in love with him . . . forever.

Charlena Gray (soon-to-be Richardson)

The End

Book Club Questions

Do you think the characters and their problems, decisions, and relationships were believable or realistic?

Which character could you relate to best and why?

Was the author clear about what he or she was trying to say, or were you confused by some of what you read? How did this affect your reading of the book?

What were some of the major themes of the book? Are they relevant in your life? Did the author effectively develop these themes?

Were you glad you read this book? Would you recommend it to a friend? Did this book make you want to read more work by this author?

Has reading this book made you think about religion or spirituality in your own life in a new or different way? How so?

How effectively does the author portray the presence of spirituality in the characters' everyday lives? Has the author succeeded in presenting faith in a way that feels relevant and relatable?

Do you think the author is trying to elicit a certain response from the reader, such as sympathy? How has this book changed or enhanced your view of the author?

Did the book seem adequately researched? Why or why not?

Thanks for your purchase. I hope you've enjoyed No Matter What.

If the ideas in this work of fiction resonated with you, checkout **The Couples Academy** and **RelationshipEDGE Mastery** Courses @ AchieversCourse.com/courses.

Algernon A. Tucker